A POWER BOYS ADVENTURE

The Mystery of
THE MILLION-DOLLAR PENNY

By Mel Lyle

Illustrated by
Raymond Burns

WHITMAN PUBLISHING COMPANY • Racine, Wisconsin

Contents

Jack Power stopped on the steep mountain path. He was stripped to the waist. Perspiration glistened on his tan shoulders. Turning and looking down at his father and brother, he said, "You know something? I'm getting kind of thirsty."

"This is like being in a jungle," Chip said, pleased by the idea. He was fifteen, two years younger than Jack. "What if we were—in a jungle—and without food and water and no help in sight?"

"Why imagine that?" Thomas Power asked. "It would be just as easy, Chip, to imagine something cool and refreshing."

Unlike his sons, Mr. Power had not removed his shirt during their hike. Black hair, streaked with premature gray, stuck damply to his forehead.

"There may be man-eating savages," Chip said, continuing the pretense he preferred.

Mr. Power moved the camera case which he carried slung over his shoulder. He kept a straight face as he said, "I hope I can get pictures of those man-eating savages before they have their lunch."

Near the top of the path, Chip passed his brother. He stopped suddenly and exclaimed, "Hey! Look up ahead! Civilization!"

Jack tried to step around Chip. "Is it a town?" he asked eagerly. "Boy, could I do with a Coke!"

"What have you fellows discovered?" Mr. Power asked.

Jack moved to one side on the narrow path. "Take a look for yourself, Dad. Some kind of an airport."

"An airport?" Mr. Power said disbelievingly. "Out here? In the Ozarks?"

"Wow, what a spot for smugglers!" Chip said. "You know, they could fly all their illegal stuff from here."

The path led to a clearing. They started across it

toward the ramshackle hangar.

Jack shook his head despondently. "This place isn't going to have a Coke machine."

"I wouldn't mind going up," Mr. Power said. "Aerial shots—I'd really like to get some."

Crickets chirped busily in the bright sunlight as the boys and their father continued walking toward the hangar. Two immense white pigs slept side by side along a fence. Chickens hopped from the skeleton of a motorless biplane that had been junked.

"Here he comes, Chip," Mr. Power announced, smiling. "The leader of those smugglers you were talking about."

A lanky young man came toward them across the clearing. Long before he reached them, he called out, "Howdy." His hair was a much brighter red than Jack's, and he had more freckles. "Mighty good day for flying," he added as he drew nearer.

"Is the pilot around?" Mr. Power asked.

"You want to go camping?" the man answered. "My name's Clay. I'm the only pilot around that I know of. Run a flying service for campers. Take you anywhere you want in Missouri, Kentucky, Tennessee,

Mississippi, Arkansas, Oklahoma, and Kansas." He laughed because he had rattled off all the states in one breath. "See that whirlybird?" He gestured with his thumb over his shoulder. "She'll set you down anyplace you want to camp, as nice and easy as a hen on a nest of eggs."

"I'm a photographer," Mr. Power said, indicating the camera slung over his shoulder.

"Well," Clay said, grinning. "Now ain't that nice!"

"Camping isn't what I had in mind. I was thinking of getting some aerial shots."

"Is it safe going up with him?" Chip whispered to Jack.

"Because he's wearing overalls?" Jack whispered back. "Is that what's bothering you?"

Chip shrugged. "He just doesn't look as if he could fly anything."

On the way to the helicopter, Chip pointed out dark, threatening clouds. They lay along the horizon like a black border.

"Don't let 'em worry you, son," Clay said. "You're not scared of flying, are you?"

"No." Chip shook his head. "Heck, no!"

Just then a growl of thunder came from the menacing horizon. Thin tendrils of lightning flashed restlessly.

"Lightning," Jack said apprehensively. Obviously, flying with Clay didn't appeal to him, either.

"Let's get airborne before I don't have enough light for a picture," Mr. Power said.

As soon as they were inside the helicopter, Chip pointed at the sturdy metal floor. "This thing is really built," he said admiringly, as though to reassure himself.

Jack read the sign over the door up front. " 'For emergency use only.' "

"Golly, are you just supposed to walk out that door in an emergency?" Chip asked. "We don't have a parachute. How could we?"

Before Jack could answer, Clay said, "I don't like the looks of that. No, siree. . . ."

Chip glanced at the helicopter's control board. It appeared very complicated. "Can't he figure it out?" Chip whispered to Jack. "I'm not surprised, because—"

Chip broke off. He realized that the others were all looking out of the windshield. He followed their eyes.

A small white plane hung high in the air, its motor sputtering.

Suddenly the sputtering sound ended. There was complete silence. . . .

"Its motor conked out!" Jack exclaimed, aghast.

No one else said anything. They all waited tensely, their eyes strained toward the plane. While it zoomed straight for the ground they watched as if paralyzed.

Seconds later, when the motor caught and the plane leveled off, they all rushed out of the helicopter for a better view of what was happening. As they stood looking up at the plane, it started to sputter again.

"You think it's out of gas?" Jack asked.

"That's what it sounds like," Chip answered, without moving his eyes from the falling plane.

This time, while still sputtering, the plane dived downward.

Chip immediately started running across the airfield in the plane's direction, and the others followed. The airfield was merely a clearing cut in the mountain brush, so when they reached the edge of the field they were stopped by a wall of growth. Then they realized that Clay had been calling to them from some distance back. They turned to face him.

"You'll never get through that," Clay drawled. "I been yellin' for you to stop. Come on back! The only way to get to that plane is to fly to it!"

Returning to the helicopter, Jack and Chip sprinted ahead of their father and Clay. As the boys clambered aboard, there was no evidence now that they were hesitant to fly with Clay. Their only thought was to rescue whoever was in the wrecked plane.

Clay flipped the ignition switch and pressed the starter button. That set off a deafening roar. The rotor blades started to turn, picking up speed until their tips, which could be seen from the cockpit, appeared to be nothing but a blur. Clay poured on more power. Then he moved a control slightly, and the helicopter lifted straight up from the ground.

In minutes, the helicopter reached a spot from which they could see smoke rising listlessly in the still air.

"You see the smoke?" Chip shouted. But he couldn't even hear himself above the roar of the rotors, so he pointed and soundlessly formed the words, "There! There!"

Clay nodded. He raised his hand, forefinger and

thumb making a circle. Soon he had the helicopter hover-
ing over the burning plane. But he veered off to the left
to find a landing place. He came down finally on the
gravelly bed of a creek.

The four of them ran single file as fast as they could
go along the creek. Jack, far in the lead, stopped to
catch his breath. The others caught up with him.

"You hear that?" Chip asked, as they all stood pant-
ing.

Though they couldn't see the plane, they could hear
the menacing crackle of flames.

"I'm going back to the 'copter," Clay told them.
"We're going to need something to put out that fire."

As soon as Clay left, Chip said, "We're not just
going to stand here and wait for him, are we?"

"If this creek weren't all dried up," Jack said, "then
we—"

"Yeah. Of course. We'd have some water to put out
the fire." Chip started off. "Come on, will you?" he
urged. "People in that plane are going to need help."

Mr. Power must have thought Chip was right, for
he pushed ahead of his sons without a word. Jack and
Chip followed close behind him.

The crackling sound of flames directed them to the plane.

Holding their hands up to shield their faces from the intense heat, they tried to approach the wreck. But immediately the heat drove them back.

Clay arrived. Mr. Power and the boys hurried toward him.

"Couldn't find an extinguisher!" Clay shouted, shaking his head. "I was sure I had one!"

"What're we going to do?" Chip asked desperately.

Mr. Power looked up at the sky. "I'm sure I felt a drop of rain," he said.

They all looked up. Then Chip yelled jubilantly. It was beginning to rain.

"A downpour is what we need," Mr. Power said.

"It's raining harder," Chip said. "A little harder."

"Why the sun's out, for crying out loud!" Jack exclaimed in disgust.

The rain suddenly came down in earnest. But it stopped as abruptly as it started—a summer shower. The sun had hardly stopped shining.

The smoke rising from the plane had turned to plumes of hissing steam. Soaked, Mr. Power, Clay, and the boys made their way hurriedly to the plane. Heat still made it difficult to approach.

They all worked at the door. The twisted frame kept it from opening, and the metal of the door was hot and hard to hold onto, even with their hands protected by their handkerchiefs.

Fanning the steam from his face, Jack looked into the cockpit. He put his head all the way in. Then he withdrew it fast, as if he had been burned.

"There's no one in there!" he shouted. "No one!"

2 *Phantom in the Flesh*

Chip took a quick look into the cockpit of the small plane. He turned to the others, a frightened expression on his face. "Jack's right!" he exclaimed.

Mr. Power and Clay also looked inside.

"Strange," Mr. Power marveled. "Even if they'd been burned, there would be remains. But there's *nothing!*"

Clay nodded agreement. "That little old plane's clean as a whistle."

"Golly!" Chip's eyes were wide. "I just thought of that ghost ship. You know, that one they came across —oh, a long, long time ago. Nobody on it. And it was a long way out on the ocean."

"Now, let's not go getting melodramatic," Jack told Chip.

"The pilot or the passengers couldn't have been thrown from the plane," Mr. Power said. "The jammed door rules that out. So the only other possibility—"

"Is that they climbed through the window," Jack interrupted excitedly.

Mr. Power nodded. "Of course. That would be the natural thing to do. With flames leaping at you, you'd move—and fast."

They all started searching about the plane for survivors. Anxiously they pushed aside the soaking wet foliage.

"I haven't even come across a footprint," Chip said.

"Are you still trying to prove this is some kind of a ghost airplane?" Jack asked Chip.

"What're you talking about? I didn't—"

"Boys!" Mr. Power admonished his sons. "Let's just concentrate on the job we've got to do!"

"How could there be footprints?" Jack said, getting in the last word. "That downpour would have washed them away."

Because of the urgent need for speed, Mr. Power suggested that Clay take the helicopter up and search from the air while they continued to look on the ground.

"Maybe we all ought to look around some more first," Jack suggested. "Farther away from the plane."

"Some prints could have been made *after* the downpour," Chip said. "They'd be around. Wouldn't they, Jack?"

"So let's find them," Jack answered, without lifting his eyes from the ground.

After more searching, Mr. Power said, "We're not doing any good looking down here. Maybe we all ought to go up with you, Clay."

"I'm for that," Jack said. "Maybe Chip wasn't so melodramatic after all. This is getting spookier by the minute."

While Clay's helicopter skimmed the tops of the trees, Mr. Power, Jack, and Chip stared intently at the ground. Clay covered a wide area systematically but without success.

After the helicopter finally settled down on a barren spot, its passengers started off in different directions.

Jack hadn't gone far when he called to Chip, "Come

here, will you? This could be something."

Chip rushed to his brother, asking, "What did you find?" And then he saw a cave, its elliptical entrance at the foot of a hillside. "You mean the cave? What's it got to do with—"

"They could have crawled in to get out of that downpour," Jack said.

"But it's not raining now."

"I know. They might have passed out, though. They *could* be in pretty bad shape, couldn't they?"

"It wouldn't be such a good idea," Chip said, shaking his head, "for us to crawl in there. I know that's what you're thinking."

"If they crawled in," Jack persisted, "they didn't go far. So we wouldn't have to, either—to find them."

"But we don't have a light or anything," Chip objected.

Jack bent down and looked into the darkness of the cave.

"You can't see anything, can you, Jack?"

"What're you so scared about? How far would somebody get who's badly hurt? Not very far. And I don't plan to go any farther."

"What was that?" Chip asked, straightening and holding himself very still.

Jack also stood motionless and silent. "I thought I heard something, too," he said finally. "It could have been Dad calling to Clay—or vice versa."

"It seemed to come from the cave, though. Didn't you think—"

Chip broke off as Jack grabbed his arm.

"Hel-l-lo!"

The faint cry came from the hillside above them. They both realized this at the same time and started running up the hill as fast as they could go.

A man lay flat on his back. The collar of his white shirt had been opened and the tie loosened. Mud and perspiration concealed the features of his face. The dark business suit he wore was torn and muddy.

Jack and Chip knelt beside him.

"Can you talk?" Jack asked.

The man's eyes opened and closed, as though he were too weak to keep them open.

"He's in pain," Chip said.

"Where are the other passengers?" Jack bent even closer to the man's face. "Did they go in the cave?"

Strangely, this question excited the man. He tried to sit up. He also shook his head. "No—no," he said weakly, falling back. "I'm—I'm the only one."

Mr. Power and Clay came running toward the boys and the pilot. The first thing Jack did was tell them that there were no passengers, that the pilot alone had been hurt.

Thunder rumbled off in the distance as he spoke.

"We've got to rush him to the hospital," Mr. Power said.

"I'll get him there," Clay drawled, "in one big hurry."

"Is it all right to move him?" Chip asked worriedly.

"We've no choice," Mr. Power said. "He can't be left here. We'll have to be careful that—"

"But, Dad," Jack pointed out, "he's already moved a lot in getting away from the burning plane."

"I know," Mr. Power said. "But we must still handle him carefully."

Clay flew the helicopter as close to the injured pilot as he could. Slowly and very gently they lifted the injured man aboard.

In no more than five minutes Clay had his helicopter

above the white buildings of the hospital in Pine Springs. From three hundred feet the buildings looked like models set on a bright green lawn that was no bigger than a postage stamp.

Soon they were low enough to see doctors and nurses crowding the windows watching the helicopter.

Clay pulled back the control stick, lessened the pitch of the blades, and the helicopter's landing gear soon settled onto the hospital lawn.

Interns, apprehensive because of the unusual arrival, came on a run with a stretcher. Quickly, expertly, they transferred the injured pilot from the helicopter to the stretcher and hurried toward the emergency entrance. A doctor appeared and took notes as he questioned Mr. Power. A crowd, meanwhile, had gathered around the helicopter.

"Hey, Jack, Chip!"

The boys turned and saw a familiar figure—Eddie Rowans—pushing his way through the crowd. The Powers were living in the Rowans farmhouse while their father worked on a picture story about caves in the Missouri Ozarks. Eddie was eighteen, a year older than Jack. His tight T-shirt and chino pants displayed his muscular build. His hair was much lighter than Chip's. It was practically white.

"What'd you do," Eddie asked, "rob a bank or something?"

"Using a helicopter for the getaway," Chip replied, grinning.

"This happens to be a hospital, not a bank," Jack reminded Eddie.

"Well, fill me in," Eddie said eagerly.

Between the two of them, Jack and Chip told Eddie all that had happened.

Mr. Power moved toward them, after the doctor had finished questioning him. "Hello, Eddie," he said. "I just tried to pay Clay for his services," he told his sons. "He said I hadn't gotten any pictures, so he wouldn't take a cent. Said it was a mission of mercy."

"You want a lift home, Mr. Power?" Eddie asked. "The wagon's parked right there at the curb." He laughed. "Of course, *I'll* charge you for the ride."

All the while there had been intermittent rumbles of thunder. As they were leaving Pine Springs, the rumbling stopped. But now black clouds which had spread from the horizon filled the sky. It became so dark that Eddie had to switch on the headlights of the station wagon.

"Looks like a bad storm coming up," Chip observed.

"No kidding," Jack said, needling his brother.

"I hope you can make it home, Eddie," Mr. Power said, "before—" He stopped speaking because Eddie had turned off onto the shoulder of the road. "What's wrong?"

Eddie pulled up hard on the hand brake. "See how light the sky is?" he said. "'Way off there. This is a twister, unless I miss my guess!"

"You mean a tornado?" Chip asked.

"I don't know what to do," Eddie said, speaking quickly, nervously. "Yeah, Chip, yeah—a tornado. What's best? What do you think, Mr. Power? Should we sit here, hoping the tornado misses us—or—or race for home?"

3 *Calm Before the Storm*

"They're worse than hurricanes, aren't they, Dad?" Chip asked. "Tornadoes?"

"Let's all be calm," Mr. Power said. "There's no need for panic. Perhaps, Eddie, if you just keep moving—don't speed. . . ."

"But, Dad," Chip said, "we're liable to ride right into the thing."

"Then again, we might not," Mr. Power pointed out. The dashboard light revealed his uncertain expression.

"Yeah, Dad, yeah. But we *might*."

"What you're forgetting, Chip," Jack said, "is that

a tornado is pretty narrow—"

"But powerful," Eddie reminded him, as he reached out and switched off the lights. "I don't want to try to make it home."

"—no more than a few hundred yards wide," Jack finished, ignoring Eddie's comment. "So if we make some time, there's a good chance we'll be out of its way. You know, before—"

"It's getting darker and darker!" Chip exclaimed.

"What do you say we go, Dad?" Jack said.

"Jack, just quiet down," Mr. Power said. "Don't get panicky. You, too, Chip."

The boys and Eddie all started talking at once, and Mr. Power had to shout to quiet them.

"All that helped me to decide," Mr. Power said with authority. "All the hubbub. We're going to stay right here!"

"But, Dad!" Jack objected.

"No, Jack, no. We're better off sitting it out. To start racing—and I'm sure that would happen in spite of what I said—would be disastrous. It's not good to panic. It never is!"

They all sat silently after Mr. Power's outburst.

Chip was the first to speak. "One thing," he said, "it's not going to get any darker than it is."

"What I wish," Jack said, "is that there'd be a little breeze or something. The air's too doggone quiet. Gives you the creeps."

"Look for the funnel," Eddie told them. "Coming down from the sky. A long funnel. I saw one once—just once. I was a little kid then. Everybody was down in the storm cellar—the whole family. And I peeked. I've never forgotten it."

Obviously changing the subject, Mr. Power said, "I wonder how our patient at the hospital is getting along. He didn't seem to have been burned."

"But he was in pain," Jack said. "You could see he was."

"That funnel, Eddie, from the sky," Chip said, changing the subject back again. "I bet it could suck up this car with all of us in it."

"Right," Eddie agreed. "And take you up higher than you ever were in that helicopter."

"I'll have to be leaving tomorrow," Mr. Power said, determinedly changing the subject once again. Only somber silence followed this announcement. After a moment, Mr. Power added, "My first stop will be the Mark Twain Cave up in the northern part of the state."

"Tornadoes are over quick," Eddie said.

"Hmmmm," Jack murmured. "Short and sweet."

"Where we ought to be is in one of those storm cellars," Chip said.

"Boys, you won't mind staying with Eddie, will you?" Mr. Power asked, still intent on speaking of something other than the tornado. "I won't be away more than a few weeks."

"Look at the windshield!" Chip exclaimed. "It's raining. It doesn't rain during a tornado, does it?"

"Who says it doesn't?" Eddie challenged.

"For once I think Chip's right," Jack said. "I don't think it does rain. Chip is right, isn't he, Dad?"

Mr. Power looked at their anxious faces. Then, clearly to relieve their fears, he answered, "Oh, yes, yes, Chip's right."

At first the raindrops made splashes against the windshield that were the size of a half dollar. They were few and far between. But the boys and Eddie welcomed them with cheers.

"No, Dad," Chip answered his father belatedly. "I

don't mind staying on at the farm while you're gone.
For a while there, listening to Eddie talk about tornadoes, I didn't know if I was going to make it—you
know, survive."

"Hey," Jack said, "it's really raining now."

The rain was coming straight down, as though
dumped from buckets. It continued to outdo itself, raining harder and harder. The roof of the station wagon
was like a huge drum being steadily pounded.

"You live here," Jack shouted to Eddie above the roar
of the rain. "What kind of storm is this?"

Mr. Power shouted that it was a cloudburst. Eddie
immediately agreed with him.

The noise of the rain made conversation too difficult.
They all sat silently, motionless, as though hypnotized.
And then, to everyone's surprise, the rain stopped
abruptly, as if it had been switched off.

"Golly!" Chip exclaimed. "I just thought of Blaze—"

"Was he staked out in back?" Jack asked with alarm.

"Of course he was," Chip answered. His worry over
their Dalmatian made him irritable. "You know he
was."

"Knock it off, you guys," Eddie said. "You think my

father would've left Blaze out there?"

"He might not have thought of him," Chip said.

"Maybe he didn't know Blaze was chained up," Jack said. "Blaze could've been drowned, the way that water was coming down."

"We know how it was coming down," Chip muttered, still very upset. "We were here, too, you know."

Eddie started the car. "Okay, fellows," he said. "The only way to find out what happened is to go home."

"Eddie's right," Mr. Power said.

As the black clouds rolled away, a luminous gray sky appeared. An unnaturally bright glow filled the air. Several times they came to ponds that filled dips in the road. Eddie had to drive through them very slowly.

They had just gone through the biggest pond and had proceeded up the hill beyond it, when off in the distance they saw a barrier across the road.

"It's a trailer truck," Chip said.

"What's it doing, turning around?" Jack asked.

They soon saw that the truck was straddling the road diagonally and wasn't moving.

"Wow!" Chip exclaimed. "Look at its front wheels! They're in mud up to the hubcaps."

"Probably skidded," Mr. Power said.

As they neared the truck, Jack said, "You'd better not pull over, Eddie. The shoulder of the road is pure mush."

Eddie stopped on the road. The driver of the truck immediately started to walk in their direction.

Chip was the first one out of Eddie's car. "I'm heading for home, Dad!" he called back.

"Chip, wait!" his father ordered, as he followed Jack and Eddie out of the car.

"I want to check on Blaze." Chip was half-turned as he spoke, but he didn't stop moving up the road. "It's not far."

"Let him go, Dad," Jack said. "He'll make it. I'll go with him, if you want me to."

As soon as his father nodded, Jack ran at a trot after Chip. He called, "Hi!" to the truck driver as he passed him. Chip was climbing through the cab of the truck to avoid going around the truck and into the mud. When Jack did the same thing, he found Chip waiting for him on the other side.

They had to do some wading, but they reached the Rowans farmhouse without serious trouble.

Blaze wasn't where they had tied him.

"I just had a feeling something had happened to him," Chip said.

"Don't panic. Remember what Dad said about panicking." Jack picked up the end of the chain. "The hound probably broke loose. Take a look at this. Come here."

Chip didn't move toward Jack. "What if he didn't break loose?" he asked in a pained monotone. *"What if he was washed away?"*

4 *Suspicions*

"Calm down," Jack said. "Do I have to keep telling you not to panic?"

"But, golly, what if Blaze was washed away?"

"But was he? We don't know that he was."

"You act as if you don't care."

Jack's shoulders rose and fell as he sighed. "All I'm trying to tell you," he said patiently, "is that we don't know what happened."

"Yeah. And you don't want me to panic. I know. I know it by heart."

As Chip started to whistle and call for Blaze, Jack told his brother that he was sure Mr. Rowans had taken care of the dog. But when they went in the back door of the farmhouse, they found the big, old-fashioned kitchen ominously quiet.

The boys looked questioningly at one another.

"I don't think Eddie's father is even here," Chip said. "So how could he have brought Blaze in out of the rain?"

"Mr. Rowans?" Jack called.

The boys stood waiting for an answer.

Jack continued to call Mr. Rowans' name as he and Chip started to go from room to room. Chip whistled occasionally and spoke Blaze's name in a coaxing way, as though the dog were playfully hiding. Finally they searched the upstairs rooms.

As they were halfway down the steps, Jack stopped suddenly.

"What's wrong?" Chip asked.

Jack just stood motionless, listening.

An unmistakable sound of movement came from the rear of the house.

"That must be Mr. Rowans!" Jack exclaimed jubilantly.

Both Jack and Chip raced down the remaining steps.

But they pulled up short at the foot of the stairs. They saw Eddie Rowans striding down the hall toward them.

"Oh, it's you," Jack said disappointedly. "I thought it was your father."

"I see you made it here okay," Eddie said. "You know what we forgot to do? It was dumb. We didn't tell you guys when you got here to phone for a tow truck."

"Did you happen to see Blaze on your way here?" Chip asked anxiously.

Eddie picked up the receiver of the phone that was in the hall. "Wait a second, Chip. Let me make this call. Blaze? No, I didn't see him. Hey," he said after a moment's wait, "this is funny. It sounds like the phone's dead. It *is* dead. What gives, Chip? You look kind of— kind of blah. . . ."

"He's worried about Blaze," Jack told Eddie.

"Your father's not around anyplace," Chip said. "We looked all over. We thought he might know what happened to Blaze."

"Eddie," Jack said with exasperation, "did you hear what Chip just said? He insists that something happened to Blaze."

"Something did." Chip thrust his face forward

challengingly. "I'm not bats. You make it sound as if I am."

Eddie raised his hands for silence. "Hey, hold it. Wait a minute."

But Chip went right on. "We found his chain broken. And that wasn't a regular rain. It was a cloudburst. So why shouldn't I think that something happened to Blaze?"

Eddie was thoughtful for a moment. "And you couldn't find my dad around?"

"Not in the house," Jack said.

Without a word, Eddie marched outside, and the boys followed him. The sun had come out. Puddles glared in the brilliant sunlight. Wet foliage glistened.

Eddie stopped before they reached the two cellar doors, set flush into the hillside. "Now that I think of it," he said, "coming here doesn't make sense. If it had been a tornado, Pop would've gone down into the storm cellar. But since it wasn't. . . ."

"Right," Jack agreed. "I didn't say anything, though, because I didn't know where you were taking us."

Chip went to the storm cellar doors anyway. He started lifting one, but it was heavy and the upper edge stuck in the frame. Jack and Eddie helped him lift the door and lay it on the ground.

"You didn't have to go knocking yourself out," Eddie told Chip. "Nobody's in there."

Nevertheless, Chip called, "Mr. Rowans!" into the darkness of the cellar.

"You want me?" a voice behind them said.

Eddie and the boys spun around. It was Mr. Rowans striding toward them. His blue work shirt was soaking wet. His drooping moustache seemed even more droopy than usual.

"We were looking for you," Eddie said.

"Now, what would I be doing down there?" Mr. Rowans gestured toward the storm cellar. He bent down and started closing the door. "No point leaving this open. Where were you boys in all that rain?"

"I'd better go make that call," Eddie said, starting off. "If the phone's still not on the blink." Eddie stopped and pointed off across a meadow. The sudden heat of the sun was causing it to steam, as the rain had done in the case of the burning plane. "Hey, guys, there's Blaze!" Eddie squatted and clapped his hands, encouraging Blaze to come to him.

The boys joined Eddie. When Blaze arrived, his tail was swishing happily. His tongue licked any face that came within range.

Chip stroked and patted Blaze roughly, but affectionately. "Where have you been?"

"Yeah, where?" Jack asked, shoving the Dalmatian playfully.

Blaze barked and leaped at the boys, getting into the spirit of the game he thought Jack and Chip were playing.

Once again Mr. Rowans came up behind them and spoke. "He came scratching at the back door. It was before all that rain came down. Probably Blaze didn't like the way it got dark any more than I did."

Blaze barked harder, as though he were contradicting Mr. Rowans.

"Quiet!" Jack yelled at him. Then he laughed.

"He broke his chain, you know," Chip told Mr. Rowans. "I'll tell you the truth. I thought he was drowned, or something."

"You see the way Blaze is acting now?" Jack said, grinning. "That's the way Chip was. I couldn't calm him down."

Just then Mr. Power came driving up between the barns. They all walked over to meet him. Eddie started to apologize for not having contacted a tow truck. Mr. Power interrupted him to explain that a mechanic with a tow truck, doing a lot of emergency work in the area, had happened along.

"I left as soon as I could get around that trailer," Mr. Power said.

"I was just over looking at my cave," Mr. Rowans told them. "There's water in it. No two ways about that. Some rockslides, too."

"Is it bad, Pop?" Eddie asked anxiously, for his father was about to realize a long-cherished dream: the opening of the cave on his property as a commercial enterprise.

"None of the slides will hurt the cave. And I'm not worried about the water. No. It'll go down." He stroked his moustache. "So I came out pretty darned good."

"This won't delay the opening of your cave?" Mr. Power asked.

Mr. Rowans shook his head. "Don't think it will."

"Pop!" Eddie exclaimed. "I forgot! You don't know about the plane that crashed. Jack and Chip were along when they flew the pilot to the Pine Springs Hospital—in a helicopter."

"Hurt bad—the pilot?" Mr. Rowans asked.

Mr. Power said, "I don't think so. But, boys, after I leave tomorrow, I think you ought to go to the hospital. See how the man is. It would be a nice thing to do."

"Right, Dad," Jack said.

"Sure," Chip echoed. "Sure thing."

The next morning, after Eddie had parked the mud-spattered station wagon in front of the hospital, no one made a move to get out.

"I wonder why Dad thought the guy would want to see us," Chip said.

"He's in a hospital, isn't he?" Jack asked. "When you're in a hospital, seeing people is just part of the whole deal."

"For all we know," Chip said, "they could be operating on him today."

"Go in and ask," Eddie suggested. "They'll tell you at the desk."

"We don't even know what his name is, come to think of it," Chip said.

"How many pilots you think were admitted in there yesterday?" Eddie asked. "And how many of those were brought by helicopter? You still think you have to know his name?"

"Come on, Chip," Jack said, getting out of the wagon. Chip followed, but Eddie remained behind the wheel.

"Aren't you coming?" Jack asked Eddie.

"I don't even know the guy," Eddie said. "At least you—"

"You know," Jack interrupted, scratching his head thoughtfully, "I'm beginning to get a funny feeling. Why are we all hesitating so much about going in to see this fellow? He's in there lying helpless in bed, and yet we're all acting chicken. Why?"

"You mean we ought to pay attention to this feeling we got about him?" Chip asked.

"I don't know," Jack said. "Could be."

Chip nodded. "Yeah. Maybe we ought to steer clear of this guy while we can."

"Come on!" Jack grabbed Chip's arm impulsively. "I like a challenge. Besides, I'm curious as to just what kind of a monster he really is."

5 *Suspicions Confirmed*

"Oh, the plane pilot," the elderly woman at the information desk said. She made it sound like the pilot was a celebrity and she knew all about him. Without checking, she said, "Mr. Craig Lewis. Room C-Three. You go straight down this hall, make a left turn, and you'll see the elevator."

Chip and Jack had the slow-moving, self-service elevator all to themselves.

"What are we going to say to him, anyhow?" Chip asked.

"You know Dad's idea. Ask him how he's feeling.

They found the door with C-3 on it. It was open, but not all the way. They tiptoed into the sunlit room without having opened the door any farther.

The two beds were made. The room was empty.

"She did say Three-C, didn't she?" Jack asked.

"C-Three," Chip corrected him. "Not Three-C."

"Well, what's on the door? I thought—"

Jack turned to check the number on the door. Before he could do so, a man in a bathrobe limped into the room.

"Yes?" The man faced them belligerently. "What is it?"

"We're looking for Mr. Lewis," Jack said.

"Excuse me." A nurse all in white came briskly into the room. She was holding a suit on a hanger. "I'm sorry for the delay, Mr. Lewis. But there was quite a bit of tailoring to be done, and—"

"Okay!" Lewis snapped. "Save the excuses. Just hand me the suit."

As soon as the nurse left, Lewis began to dress. Ignoring Jack and Chip completely, he concentrated on getting into his clothes in a hurry. He dropped the coat once in his rush.

The boys were uncomfortable. They didn't know what to do.

Chip finally broke the silence. "How're you feeling?" he asked hesitantly.

At least that made Lewis aware of their existence. "What was it you wanted?" he demanded as he stuffed his shirttails into his trousers.

"All we wanted was to see how you were," Jack said, suddenly angry at the man's rudeness. "We helped get you to the hospital yesterday."

"Yeah," Chip said, having caught his brother's anger. "And we sure went to a lot of trouble."

"Oh," Lewis said as he finished tightening his belt. He had a thin face and quickly moving dark eyes. He nodded, as though he now knew what they had been talking about. He turned away. When he came back, he had an open wallet and was taking bills out of it.

"Golly," Chip said, "I didn't mean we wanted money."

"Here!" Lewis insisted. And as he shoved the money at Chip, he said, "Take it!"

Chip shook his head and backed away.

In following Chip, Lewis lost his balance. He grabbed

Jack's arm to keep from falling.

After regaining his balance, he moved away from Jack, limping. "These hick doctors! They say my ankle's just slightly sprained. But what do they know?" He sat on the edge of the bed. "That's all they came up with, after keeping me here all night for observation."

"What do you say we go, Chip?" Jack said.

"What's wrong with you two?" Lewis asked in an attempt to make up to them. He even smiled. "Why don't you want my dough? It's green. It's good."

Jack shrugged. "Well. . . . Some things you just don't expect to be paid for."

Lewis nodded, grinning. His black eyes glistened brightly. "That's real noble," he said. "You live around here?"

"Until my father finishes taking some pictures—"

"Pictures?" Lewis said. "What kind of pictures?"

"Of caves and—"

"Caves!" Lewis exclaimed, startled. His eyes moved about as though he were trapped. Then he smiled. "I jumped that way, because that's what I'm interested in. Caves."

"You a spelunker?" Jack asked.

"Well, I'm in one big hurry to get down in a cave. It's my hobby. Soon as the business office checks me out of here, that's where I'm heading."

"You know that cloudburst yesterday," Chip said. "It flooded caves. . . . But the water will go down in a hurry," he added as Lewis' expression turned grim.

Moments later the boys said good-bye to the pilot and left, relieved to have the visit end. As they stepped into the hall, Chip stooped and picked up a penny.

"Good luck," he commented with a grin.

"Finding a ten-dollar bill is even better luck," Jack said, laughing.

When the boys returned to Eddie, waiting patiently in the station wagon, he wanted to know what had happened. They gave him a quick rundown.

After Chip mentioned that Lewis was a spelunker and in a big hurry to get down in a cave, Eddie said, "Who's he going with? He's not going by himself, is he?"

"Far as I know, he is," Chip answered. "He didn't mention going with anybody else, did he, Jack?"

Jack didn't have to answer, because Eddie exploded, "The guy's a phony! He's no spelunker!"

"I wouldn't trust him farther than I could *throw* a good-sized cave," Jack said. "But I don't get it. I mean, why do you say he's not a spelunker?"

"Look," Eddie said, "if you're a spelunker, you just don't go in a cave by yourself. It's too doggone dangerous. And going with two people is better yet. You've got somebody with you, and if something dangerous comes up, then you've—you've got half a chance."

"Nobody's disagreeing with you," Chip said.

"I'm not," Jack said. "I know that."

"I've got a swell idea." Eddie's eyes lit up and he snapped his fingers. "That so-called spelunker's got to come out that door. What do you say we follow him? See what he's got cooking."

Jack shook his head without saying anything.

"Eddie, tell me if I'm wrong," Chip said. "Didn't Jack say something about liking challenges?"

"Dad just left," Jack reminded his brother. "Do we have to go rushing to get into a mess?"

"Here comes Lewis," Chip said, "limping right out of that door, Eddie, just as you said he would."

"I'll let him get half a block ahead of us," Eddie said, "and then—"

"What's this going to get you, anyhow?" Jack said.

"Keep alert, man," Eddie answered, grinning. "This could be fun."

"He's walking pretty fast," Chip said. "That bum ankle mustn't be hurting him a lot because it doesn't slow him down."

Eddie started the car and drove along slowly behind Lewis. When the pilot turned at the first corner, Eddie turned. There were no other cars moving along the quiet street. As though sensing he was being followed, Lewis slowed down. He turned suddenly and looked back toward them.

"Keep going!" Jack ordered Eddie. "Don't stop!"

At the same time, Jack and Chip, riding in the front seat, bent forward to keep Lewis from seeing them.

Finally Eddie said, "Okay. I've passed him. Come up for air, you guys."

"We sure blew that," Jack said, straightening up.

"Lewis must have a guilty conscience," Chip said. "Why else would he think someone was following him?"

"You want me to tell you why?" Jack asked.

Chip nodded. "Yeah," he said. "Do you know?"

"Wouldn't it seem funny to you," Jack said, "if you were walking along and you suddenly realized a car was moving along slowly behind you? You turn, and it turns. And it keeps going along behind you in this same slow way."

"I know I did a terrible job of tailing him," Eddie said. "Is that what you're saying?"

"Yeah." Jack laughed. "I guess I was."

It was after they arrived home and were finishing lunch that Chip produced the penny he had found in the hospital hall.

Eddie reached across the round kitchen table and grabbed the coin. "Let me see it!" he exclaimed. He studied the coin for just a moment, and then he whistled. "You know what this is?"

"A penny?" Chip guessed, smiling. "How many guesses do I—"

He broke off short because a shadow suddenly moved across the table. And he saw the look of surprise on the faces of Eddie and Jack.

Chip turned in his chair, not knowing what to expect to see behind him.

6   *"We Meet Again"*

Mr. Lewis grinned, but there was a strange glint in his eyes. "Well," he said, "we meet again."

Jack, Chip, and Eddie just stared at the man. They were speechless, as though they had been caught at something they shouldn't be doing.

"You boys know if Rowans is around? Is he your father?"

Lewis had directed both questions to all of them. Eddie answered. "He's *my* father."

The way Eddie and the boys glanced at one another made it clear what they were thinking: Lewis had come to complain that they had been following him.

But Lewis said to Eddie, "Your father's a guide, isn't he?"

"What do you want him to do?" Eddie asked. "Show you through his cave?"

"Just tell him I'm here, will you?" Lewis said irritably. He began to pace the floor, in spite of his limp. The pain of his injured ankle made him wince once or twice.

After Eddie went to get his father, Chip said, just to make conversation, "The cave might still be flooded, you know. That was a lot of rain."

Lewis paused in his pacing. "You two kids," he said in his usual unfriendly way. "You know anything about caves?"

"Spelunking isn't going to be easy for you, I know that," Chip said.

"What do you mean?" Lewis demanded.

"Your ankle. It hurts, doesn't it? So it's going—"

"We don't know enough to be guides," Jack broke in on Chip. "Isn't that what you were trying to find out?"

"Maybe," Mr. Lewis admitted grudgingly, his little black eyes darting about. He started pacing again.

"That was a mistake, you know," Chip said.

Lewis stopped short. "What?" he asked irritably.

"Don't listen to my brother," Jack advised Lewis.

"Come on," Lewis said to Chip. His coaxing gesture urged him to speak. "Tell me. I want to know what mistake I made."

"You were thinking of going into a cave by yourself, weren't you?" Chip said. "And that's something you shouldn't even think about."

"Is that so?" Lewis said with heavy sarcasm. "You don't think I ought to—"

He broke off because he saw Eddie and Mr. Rowans arrive at the back door.

While Eddie was introducing his father to Lewis, Jack took Chip aside. "What's the big idea?" he asked in a whisper. "You trying to get Lewis sore?"

"Him? *Get* him sore? You don't have to *try.*"

"Shhh. He'll hear you."

Eddie came over. "Come on," he said conspiratorially. "Let's go upstairs."

When they reached Eddie's bedroom he stopped with his hand on the knob of the closed door.

"What's going on?" Chip asked.

"Be real quiet," Eddie whispered. "And we better go

in as quietly as we possibly can."

"Will you tell me what gives?" Chip exclaimed. Now both Eddie and Jack shushed him. "Okay. Okay. You don't have to jump down my throat."

Eddie stopped the boys just inside the door. He closed the door behind them, lifted a hand, and whispered, "We'll stay right here."

Soon they heard the voices of Mr. Rowans and Lewis rising from the open grating in the floor. A heater in the room under the grating provided heat for the bedroom in cold weather.

"I'll tell you what I want," Lewis was saying. "Someone to show me all the caves in this vicinity."

"All the caves?" Mr. Rowans asked.

"Well, maybe not all. But there's a certain place in one of them that I want to see." There was a pause. "That's the color of my dough. I got plenty of it and I'll pay you plenty."

"I—I—feel like sneezing," Chip whispered, his forehead furrowed and his nose twitching.

"Stop horsing around," Jack told him.

Chip couldn't protest that this was the real thing. His head had already gone back in the second phase of a sneeze. He struggled to restrain the final blast.

Jack and Eddie grabbed him, rushed him to the bed. They all dived face down as they smothered the noise of Chip's sneeze in the pillow. They lay motionless for a long time on the bed, listening for a possible reaction downstairs to the noise they had made.

But there was just silence. The voices coming up through the grating had stopped.

"Probably heard us," Jack said. "They must have gone off to talk someplace else."

"I couldn't help it," Chip complained, as they all got up off the bed. "If you have to sneeze—"

"Yeah." Jack nodded. "Of course. But you sure picked a great time."

Eddie suddenly remembered the coin Chip had found in the hospital. He dug it out of the pocket of his chinos, along with a pocket magnifying glass that swung in and out of a black plastic case.

"You know what you found, Chip?" he said. "An Indian Head cent—1864. And I'm telling you, it's rare."

"No kidding," Chip said. "What'd I tell you, Jack? Finding a penny *is* good luck."

"Here it is," Eddie went on as he looked at the penny through the magnifying glass. "An 'L.' That's the designer's initial."

"Oh, yeah. Is that good?"

"Man, I can see you know nothing, but nothing, about collecting." Eddie walked over to his desk. "I wouldn't mind having this."

"Keep it, then," Chip said. "It's yours. I'm no coin collector."

"You sound like Lewis," Jack said. "Our pal. Always flashing his money at people."

"And that's not easy," Chip said, laughing, "when all you have is a penny."

"Man, oh, man," Eddie said. He was looking at the penny through the magnifying glass. "This is really something."

"What did you find?" Chip asked. "Another initial on the other side?"

"It'd be nice," Jack said, "if that penny was a five-dollar gold piece in disguise."

Eddie stood up. He gave Jack the glass and had him sit down at the desk for a look at the penny.

"What do you see?" Eddie asked eagerly the instant

that Jack started to examine it.

Jack shrugged as he continued to look through the glass. "What am I supposed to see? I'm telling you, when Chip said he wasn't a coin collector, he was speaking for me, too."

Eddie bent over Jack's shoulder. He took the magnifying glass from him. "Just look real close," he said, slowly moving the glass away from the penny to get the strongest possible magnification.

"Yeah," Jack said. "I see what you mean now."

"What do you see?" Eddie asked.

Chip was leaning over his brother's shoulder, too. "That's what I'd like to know," he said. "How about giving me a look?"

"Let me hold the glass," Jack said. As soon as Eddie turned the glass over to him, he moved it up and down, getting what he was looking at into focus. "It looks to me like a ball with a tube in it."

"Will you let me see the thing?" Chip said. "After all, I found it."

"You're right, Jack." Eddie agreed eagerly, ignoring Chip. "Only I thought of it as shaped like a bone, cut in half."

"Well, yeah," Jack said, looking through the glass, "you could think of it that way."

"And you see all those little shapes," Eddie asked, "inside the circle or the end of the bone part?"

"Yeah, I see them."

"Come on, will you let me take a look?" Chip begged once again.

As Jack arose from the chair and turned the glass over to Chip, he said, "But what do all these hiero-glyphics mean, anyhow?"

"You got me," Eddie said. "I don't dig it."

"Whoever did this," Chip said, studying the penny under the glass, "sure did a great job. Wow!"

Eddie pointed out that there were engravers who could put the Gettysburg Address on the head of a pin.

"And, you know," he added with a laugh, "they still have loads of room left for Abe Lincoln's signature."

They were trying to figure out what the symbols on the penny might mean and speculating as to who might have lost the penny when Chip called Eddie and Jack over to the window.

Eddie's father and Lewis were cutting diagonally across a field. Both men wore pumpkin-colored hard

hats. Lewis wasn't in his business suit now, but in cover-alls.

"They're going to the cave!" Eddie exclaimed. "Let's follow them!"

"Lewis might not go for that," Jack objected. "I mean, the way we always seem to be following him."

"But this time it's different," Eddie said, grinning. "We'll be tailing him in a cave. What's the guy up to, anyhow? He's not crawling in caves for the love of it."

"True." Chip nodded. "True. I agree."

Eddie outfitted the boys with hard hats and flashlights. Chip unchained Blaze. It wasn't until then that they wondered if taking Blaze along was such a good idea. The dog came back when Chip whistled for him, but as soon as he realized Chip intended chaining him up again, he went bounding off in the direction Mr. Rowans and Lewis had taken.

When Eddie and the boys reached the cave, Blaze was already there and barking furiously.

"What's got into him?" Jack wondered aloud.

Chip tried to get Blaze to go into the cave, coaxing him and snapping his fingers. He then grabbed the Dalmatian's collar, but the dog held back.

"What're you dragging him for?" Jack complained. "We didn't want him to come in the first place, remember?"

Chip let go of Blaze's collar. "What gets me is why he's raising such a fuss."

"Maybe the hound just doesn't like caves," Jack said.

"Could be," Chip agreed. "Then again, maybe he's trying to warn us."

"What about?" Eddie asked.

Blaze sat looking up at them, moving his head from one to another as though following their conversation.

"Maybe we ought to ask him," Chip said. "Blaze. Come on. Give. What've you got against our going into the cave?"

Realizing that he was being spoken to, Blaze responded with two sharp barks.

"Well, now you know," Eddie said, and laughed. "Let's get going. I want to catch up with Pop and Lewis."

Eddie and Jack entered the mouth of the cave. Chip started to follow, but Blaze streaked to him. The Dalmatian grabbed Chip's trouser leg with his teeth and held on.

7   *The Legend of the Caves*

Jack and Eddie came rushing out of the cave. Not until then did Blaze let go of Chip's trouser leg.

"I thought of something," Chip said. "Why Blaze is acting this way. The cave could still be flooded because of the cloudburst."

Eddie shook his head. "Aw, no," he said. "There's nothing Pop doesn't know about caves. And he sure wouldn't have taken Lewis in if it was flooded."

"How about quicksand?" Chip asked.

"What about it?" Eddie wanted to know.

"I just thought," Chip said, "that all that water might —you know, make—make quicksand."

Jack scoffed at that idea. And he pointed out that if there were quicksand in the cave, Blaze couldn't know about it without having been inside.

"This is what I still think," Jack concluded, laughing. "Blaze just doesn't like caves, so he doesn't want us to, either."

However, there was a hollow ring to Jack's laughter. And as Jack, Chip, and Eddie moved ahead into the darkness of the cave, Blaze's barking reverberated ominously, warningly, behind them.

Eddie flashed his light over the walls. "Did I tell you that Pop calls his cave the Ozark Caverns? 'Cavern' sounds like a bigger deal than 'cave.' And he put in all these gravel paths and the electric wiring—which is just about done—for the lights."

"Look at that," Chip said, pointing. "Wow!"

Ahead of them, clear crystal rock rose in a formation resembling a cathedral of glass.

"Has your father fixed up the whole cave?" Jack asked. "I mean, has he made all of it civilized for the tourists?"

"Are you kidding?" Eddie said. "There are parts of this cave even he hasn't been in."

"Real rugged places, huh?" Jack said.

"You never know when you're liable to come to an eighty-foot drop—stuff like that," Eddie told him. "Pop fixed it so tourists can't get through to where it's dangerous."

"No sign of your father and Lewis," Chip said. Then he added quickly, "I didn't mean they went over one of those eighty-foot drops."

"Maybe we'd better keep quiet," Eddie said. "Lewis —and Pop—probably wouldn't like our being in here."

"You think Blaze stopped barking?" Chip asked. "You can't hear him. I don't, anyway."

"Yeah, yeah," Eddie said. "But I hear you. How about all of us quieting down?"

They proceeded more slowly and carefully into the cave's interior. The crystal wall gradually changed to a pinkish-red color.

All of a sudden Eddie flung his arms wide, stopping Jack and Chip who were on either side of him. At the same time, he excitedly whispered to them to turn off their flashlights.

They stood perfectly still in the pitch black darkness. Far in front of them and on a higher level the lights of two carbide lamps flickered like distant stars.

"Is that them?" Chip whispered.

"Okay, turn your flashlights back on," Eddie said, ignoring Chip's question. "Keep 'em pointed down, though. They're not looking back this way, but they will be if we make any noise."

Jack added, "Chip, watch that you don't trip over something."

"And don't you," Chip snapped back in a low voice. They walked on tiptoes.

A sharp rapping sound above them caused Eddie to exclaim, "What was that?"

"A rock or something bounced off my crash helmet," Jack whispered.

"Be a little more careful," Chip said.

Jack snorted in disgust.

They turned off their flashlights when they were still fifty feet from Mr. Rowans and Lewis.

The carbide light on Lewis' hard hat moved with quick jerks in the darkness.

"What's Lewis doing?" Chip asked. "Looking for something?"

"Seems as if he's in a hurry, too," Jack said.

"Maybe he's searching for the loot from one of Jesse James's holdups" whispered Eddie. "According to stories I've heard, James left loaded saddlebags in one of the caves and was shot before he could return to get them.

"Lewis isn't the first guy," Eddie finished, "who's tried to find those saddlebags." He tensed. "Did you hear that? It sounded—"

"It was a moan." Chip broke in on Eddie. "Like somebody's hurt. Listen!"

But the sound was not repeated. Eddie, Jack, and Chip stood motionless, listening for several minutes. Eddie's father and Lewis also seemed to be listening. Their carbide lights were absolutely still.

In the complete silence, a shriek of pain arose. Startled, Jack jerked back. He tripped in the darkness. In trying to keep from falling, he dislodged a rock. This freed a small stream of gravel. The rolling, sliding sound drowned out the bloodcurdling scream.

Eddie and the boys each remained frozen in position. It was clear that the men's attention had been directed their way by the sound Jack had caused.

After a time, Chip whispered irritably, "Jack, why'd

you go tripping over your feet? We're just lucky that they can't see us!"

"Listen!" Jack said warningly.

More moans began to echo through the cavern. This time as soon as one died down, another arose.

"Yipes!" Chip exclaimed.

"Shhhh," Jack warned. And then once again he said, "Listen." A spectral voice was speaking. It sounded like an eerie voice in an echo chamber.

"No! No!" the voice said pleadingly. "Don't shoot!"

A moment of complete silence followed this plea. Then there came again the groans of someone in mortal pain. It sounded as though the person who had begged not to be shot *had* been.

"Let's get out of here!"

The exclamation echoed from the walls of the cave. It took a moment for the boys to realize that it was Lewis who had spoken. Then they saw distant carbide lights moving toward them.

"Come on," Eddie said. "We don't want Lewis to know we've been spying on him."

In all the rush, Chip tripped. "Now we're even," he told Jack. "What was all that spooky noise about?"

But Eddie didn't give them a chance to talk. He herded them to one side, far off the graveled walks installed by Mr. Rowans.

"Eddie," Chip objected, "we're getting in mud."

"I know it," Eddie shot back. "But we can wait here. They won't see us."

"All that groaning's stopped," said Jack. "You notice?"

"Yeah," said Eddie. After a minute he added, "Pop better not start flashing his torch around or we're sunk."

"Why would he do that?" Jack asked.

"He just likes to look at his cave, that's why. If you fixed a place up the way my father has—"

"And how about that cloudburst?" Chip interrupted. "He might want to check on the mud back here."

Once again Eddie advised them to be quiet. They waited as the two lights drew closer and closer.

"I just hope I don't have to sneeze," Chip said.

"No pillow here," Jack told him. "But there's plenty of mud to put your face in. Shhh. . . ."

They watched in silence as Mr. Rowans and Lewis passed them and disappeared around a corner. Even then they didn't move.

"We'd better wait," Eddie warned the boys, "until they're all the way out."

While they waited, Eddie told them that according to the Jesse James legend, James had actually shot one of his pursuers in the course of hiding the saddlebags.

"You mean that what we heard was this guy's ghost telling old Jesse not to shoot him?" Chip asked incredulously.

"I don't know," Eddie said. "Do you have a better explanation for that moaning—and all the rest?"

"I wonder if this could've been what was bothering Blaze," Chip said.

"We can get going now, can't we, Eddie?" Jack asked.

Eddie turned his flash on. Jack and Chip did, too.

As they made their way out of the cave, Eddie said, "Dogs can sense a lot of stuff that people can't."

"I'm glad all those noises have stopped," Chip commented. "They were awful."

"Hmmm," Eddie agreed. "They were sure weird."

After supper that night, they sat around in the parlor of the farmhouse. The television set was on, but no one was paying any attention to the burly wrestlers on the screen who were both complaining to the referee that they were being mistreated.

"What's the matter, Pop?" Eddie said. "The cave's not flooded. What are you so glum about?"

Mr. Rowans thoughtfully stroked his droopy moustache. Finally he said, "Might as well tell you. I'm thinking I'll have to postpone the cave opening."

"Why, Pop?" Eddie said. "I thought everything was set."

Mr. Rowans told them then about the strange noises in the caves. They acted surprised, as if it were the first they had ever heard of such a thing. He said that though he wanted publicity, he didn't want a rumor to get started that the Ozark Caverns were inhabited by ghosts. Such a rumor would frighten away more customers than it would attract.

"What're you going to do, Pop?" Eddie asked.

"Do?" Mr. Rowans stroked his moustache again thoughtfully. "Maybe I'll take Mr. Lewis up on that offer he made me. He asked me to postpone the opening awhile. Said he had plenty of money and would like to charter the cave to have it all to himself. Said you chartered a boat that way, so why not a cave?"

"And what'd you tell him?" Eddie asked.

"I said I'd call off the opening for just one day—no more'n that. The mud that cloudburst stirred up will have a chance to dry out a bit."

"Did he show you his money, Mr. Rowans?" Chip asked. "I'm just curious."

"Well, he did take out his wallet. And I'll say it looked mighty stuffed."

Jack, who had remained thoughtfully silent, suddenly sprang up. "Something just occurred to me," he said excitedly. "Those noises in the cave. Lewis wanted the opening postponed. Maybe he made them so that—"

Mr. Rowans shook his head and also stood up. "Oh, no, Jack," he said. "I was right beside Lewis all the time. All that moaning and carrying on surprised him as much as it did me."

Jack shrugged. "Well," he said, "it was an idea."

"We really shouldn't be talking about Lewis. I rented him a room, you know, which makes him a guest." Mr. Rowans stretched and yawned. "Guess I'll be turning in. You ought to be thinking about it, too. It's getting late." He paused in the doorway and looked back.

"Jack and Chip, maybe I should tell you that your father asked me to keep an eye on you. So don't you let Eddie get you into any mischief."

The second Mr. Rowans was gone, Jack went into a huddle with the other boys. He suggested that Lewis might have rigged up some kind of electronic gadget which made all those spooky sounds.

"He had enough reason to," Jack finished, "since he wanted the cave all to himself."

"You think he really might be out to find that stuff Jesse James—"

"I don't know about that," Jack interrupted his brother. "But he's looking for something."

"Remember what my father said," Eddie reminded Jack and Chip. "I'm not supposed to get you in a mess."

At that moment a knock sounded at the front door. It was a slow, menacing kind of knock that would have gone with the spectral voice they had heard in the cave! It was followed by a heavy silence.

Eddie and the boys looked at one another as if to say, "Who could this be—so late at night?" No one moved.

8   *The Million-Dollar Penny*

"How about answering the door?" Jack said at last. He implied that either Eddie or Chip should answer it, since they were standing and he wasn't.

Eddie and Chip hesitated. Each waited for the other to go to the door. The knock sounded again, in the same slow, ominous way. Both boys started for the door at the same time.

When they reached it, they hesitated again. "Go ahead, Chip," Eddie said. "Go on, open it."

Chip opened the door. But he opened it slowly and not very wide. What he saw caused him to step back, startled.

Moonlight tinged the darkness with a greenish glow. Blaze, staked near the barn, started to bay mournfully. A stranger stood in the doorway—a tall, gaunt man with lank, light brown hair and a bony face. His overall appearance gave the disquieting suggestion of a Frankenstein monster.

"Terribly sorry," the man said, "to be disturbing you at this time of night." His precise and formal diction made him seem all the more strange. "I took a wrong turn, which delayed me." And as he came into the kitchen, he asked, "May I come in? I know it's terribly late, but I've come about sixty miles. And I saw the light on, so—"

"Sure," Chip said uncertainly. "Come in."

By this time Jack had walked over to his brother and Eddie.

The man noticed their silence. Perhaps he took it for embarrassment, for he smiled and introduced himself. He was Sven Beestrom. The boys nodded and muttered that they were glad to know him, but they didn't tell him their names. They didn't offer to shake hands, either. It was as though they all felt the same need to keep a safe distance from him.

"I'm a paleontologist," Beestrom said.

Silence greeted this announcement. No one seemed to know what to do or say next. Even Blaze had stopped his baying.

"It shouldn't surprise you," Beestrom said, "that since I'm a paleontologist I'm searching for bones and arti-facts."

"In the caves, you mean?" Chip blurted out.

The gaunt face nodded. "And it's been my experience that the natives of a locality can give you invaluable information. So I stop at farmhouses and make inquiries—just as I'm doing here. Besides, I heard of the Rowans cave and—"

"Jack, you think that engraving—you know—the bone on the penny. . . ."

Chip stopped because of the look that came over Jack's face. He recognized it as the look Jack used to let his brother know he'd opened his mouth when he shouldn't have.

"I don't understand your reference to a penny," Beestrom said, his tone both puzzled and exaggeratedly formal.

Without a word, Eddie produced the penny and his

pocket magnifying glass. Then he pointed out the engraving that resembled one end of a bone.

"Amazing, *most* amazing," Beestrom said, nodding his head as he continued to look at the engraving. "This could be a clue to a decidedly important find. On the other hand, it might be meaningless. But one can't afford to overlook any possible lead." He paused a moment and looked at them thoughtfully. "I just thought of a folk tale I heard in a little Ozark mountain store, about a vanished race. In the 1800's some evidence concerning them was discovered by natives of this area and, according to this tale, the whereabouts of their remains was recorded on metal. This penny's metal, of course. But I doubt very much that the inscription on it is related to that folk tale. Still, it might be. And in my profession, as I've said, one must follow every clue."

Beestrom's excitement communicated itself to Eddie and the boys. It made them forget their first unfavorable reaction to the gaunt man. He told them excitedly that the markings on the coin might represent stalactites and stalagmites, serving as landmarks in pinpointing a certain location in a cave.

"It's a matter," he said, "of finding precisely such

an arrangement of stalactites and stalagmites. And that, I fear, would be like trying to find the proverbial needle in the proverbial haystack."

"Well, if we come across it," Eddie said, "we'll let you know."

Beestrom left after making an impression of the engraving by placing a piece of paper over it and rubbing the paper with a lead pencil.

"You know what I'm wondering?" Jack said as soon as the door had closed on Beestrom. "I'm wondering who made that engraving on the penny."

"Must have been someone interested in—" Eddie broke off. "What was that Beestrom said he was?"

"But how could it have been a paleontologist?" Jack said. "You know where Chip found the penny. Unless there was a paleontologist in the hospital."

"Why not?" Chip demanded. "They're human, aren't they—those paleontologists?"

"Beestrom doesn't look too human," Eddie said.

"We're forgetting that whole folk tale angle," Chip said. "That engraving could have been made any time within the last hundred years."

After they went upstairs they continued talking.

There were three beds in the large, moonlight-flooded room.

"Eddie," Jack said, "I know how to get those so-called spirits out of your father's cave. We could take a look in Lewis' room. If we spot some electronic stuff, we'll know Lewis is to blame. Some sound equipment. Any evidence of—"

"I thought ghosts were making all that racket," Chip said. "Man, you're disillusioning me."

"It's people like you," Jack told Chip, "who go around making legends."

"Well," Chip said, laughing, "making 'em up is a good way to kill time, isn't it?"

Jack didn't answer.

After a long silence, Eddie said, "I'll tell you what Pop really needs. Publicity. Something that'll really pull in the tourists."

"Maybe this ghost bit would be okay," Jack said.

"Could be," Eddie answered, "but I doubt if Pop would think so."

"Your dad might be wrong, you know," Jack said. "Maybe it wouldn't scare away people the way he thinks."

"Yeah," Eddie pointed out, "but he'd be risking a lot to find out."

They tried to think of some surefire publicity angle.

"If we only had a cave over three thousand feet down," Eddie said wistfully. "A real record-breaker, deeper than that one in France."

"Or the tallest something," Jack said. "Or the biggest—"

"How about white bats?" Chip said.

"White bats?" Eddie echoed incredulously.

"Yeah," Chip said.

"There's no such thing, is there, Eddie?" Jack asked.

"I didn't say there was," Chip protested. "But if there were any, and the only place they hung out was in the Ozark Caverns—"

"Hey, I want to sleep," Jack said.

"Me, too," Eddie agreed sleepily.

"I still think," Chip persisted, "that something like white bats would be good. Not white bats, because there aren't any, but something. . . . How about that engraving on the penny?"

Jack flopped over noisily on his bed.

"What if it wasn't a key just to some old bones—of

a vanished race?" Chip went on. "What if it was a key to something even more sensational that would really make the cave famous?"

"How?" Jack murmured.

"I don't know. I'm just dreaming."

"Hmmm. How about letting *us* dream?"

The next morning Eddie showed his father the penny Chip had given him. While he was telling him that it might somehow bring publicity to the cave, Lewis came down for breakfast. Mr. Rowans was looking at the penny through Eddie's magnifying glass.

"An old coin?" Lewis said. When he moved, it was plain that his limp was completely gone now. "Give me a look."

Mr. Rowans turned the magnifying glass and penny over to Lewis.

As Lewis looked at the penny, he said, "You know, I'm a collector."

"So's Eddie," Mr. Rowans told Lewis. "You should see his collection. Keeps each coin in an envelope. All the facts about it are written right on the envelope."

"I'd like this one, Eddie," Lewis said. "What do you

say? Would you sell it to me?"

Eddie shook his head. "I want it," he said. "Besides, Chip gave it to me as a gift, and—"

"Two hundred bucks?" Lewis said and took his wallet out and opened it up. "What do you say to two hundred bucks?"

The boys stared at Lewis in astonishment.

"I told you," Eddie said, "it was given to me—as a gift."

"Yeah. I know you told me. I'll raise the ante to five hundred. Okay?"

"That's a pile of money," Mr. Rowans murmured.

Eddie shook his head again. "Why are you so anxious to get that coin?" he asked suspiciously.

"All right," Lewis said irritably. "A thousand! That's it. I'm not topping that."

Mr. Rowans cleared his throat nervously.

"A thousand?" Eddie repeated disbelievingly.

"I thought that would interest you," Lewis said, and he started pulling bills from the wallet.

Eddie immediately turned to Chip and insisted he take the penny. "If it's worth that much," he said, holding the penny extended to him, "you shouldn't have given it to me. Go on. Take it. It's up to you whether you want to sell it or not."

"But I gave it to you," Chip said.

"Sure," Eddie answered, "but at the time it was just something you'd found and—"

"You found it, huh?" Lewis said.

Chip nodded. "When we came up to see you."

"I figured as much," Lewis said. "Right off, I knew it was mine. Soon as I saw it."

"Yours?" Chip said disbelievingly.

"Where'd you find it?" Lewis asked. "I looked all over—"

"Out in the hall," Chip answered. "Come to think of it, it was just outside of your room."

"That was the one place I didn't look," Lewis said, as he reached out and took the penny from Eddie.

9 *"Call Me Chuck"*

"You see," Lewis said with a grin, "when I was bidding for that penny, I knew it was mine. I knew it all along. But I didn't mind paying the dough. I figured it like a reward. So who gets it?" Lewis pointed at Chip. "You?"

Chip shook his head.

"You found it," Eddie said. "Didn't you, Chip?"

"I don't want any reward for finding a penny," Chip told Lewis.

When Lewis tried to force money on Chip, he kept shaking his head and wouldn't take it.

Lewis and Mr. Rowans left shortly after that. They

both wore the pumpkin-colored hard hats and coveralls they had worn the other time. Blaze ran ahead of them. Jack, Chip, and Eddie stood outside watching them disappear in the deep shadow of a distant woods.

"What's Blaze going for?" Chip asked. "We know he doesn't like caves."

"You should have taken that reward," Eddie said to Chip, ignoring Chip's comment.

Chip shrugged. "I don't know. Maybe I should've."

"A thousand for just a penny," Eddie marveled. "Even for a rare 1864 Indian Head cent, that's still real money."

"You know what's bothering me now?" Chip said.

"That you didn't take those thousand clams?" Eddie asked.

"Oh, no. I'm wondering if he really did lose that penny—that's what I'm wondering. He—he said he did. But how do we know?"

"Right," Eddie agreed enthusiastically. "And when did he say it was his? It wasn't until you said you'd found it in the hospital."

Chip shook his head dispiritedly. He kicked at the trunk of the towering oak under which they stood.

Until then, Jack had been silent and thoughtful. Now he said, "If that penny does belong to Lewis, how about the engraving on it? Has it got something to do with what he's looking for in the cave?"

"What do you want to do, follow him again?" Eddie asked.

"Maybe we'd better, Jack," Chip said. "This time the guy's liable—"

"He's no paleontologist like Beestrom." Jack went right on, pursuing his own thoughts. "So he's not looking for bones."

"How do we know?" Chip objected. "Face it, we don't know very much about Lewis. I've got an idea. Look. You can't even see him or Mr. Rowans now. They're out of sight. Now's our chance to take that look in Lewis' room."

"Right," Jack said and turned toward the house.

Chip ran ahead and kept the lead all the way to the room. He tried the door. "Hey," he said, shaking the knob. "It's locked."

Eddie slapped his hand to his head. "Oh, I forgot. Lewis asked Pop for a key."

"Isn't there another one?" Jack asked.

"Not that I know of," Eddie said. "I remember now, Pop saying that he'd need the key to get in to clean the room. And Lewis answered that he'd take care of all the cleaning that had to be done."

"There must be something important in there," Chip said. "Otherwise, why is Lewis so anxious to keep people out?"

"Yeah," Eddie said, nodding his head profoundly.

"You guys are forgetting one very, *very* important thing," Jack said.

"What's that important?" Chip asked.

"Lewis' stuff," Jack said. "Or, rather, the fact that he doesn't have any. Remember? It was all burned up in the plane."

"Sure." Chip rattled the knob again. "But you see the door's locked, don't you? That's something *you* forgot, Jack. Why's he got it locked if he doesn't have something in there he doesn't want anybody to see?"

When Jack and Chip started talking about getting in through a window, Eddie was against it.

"I know what Pop would say," Eddie explained. "Lewis is a guest here. We've got no business going into his room."

"I can see that applying to you," Jack said. "I mean since your dad's renting the room to Lewis. But Chip and I—"

"Yeah," Chip said, "it would be all right for us to bust in."

Jack grinned. "Perfectly all right."

They went around the house to the window to Lewis' room. When they got there, Jack said there was no point in both of them going in.

"You call it," Jack said. "Odd or even."

"Even," Chip said, as he and Jack dropped their right arms simultaneously.

Chip had one finger extended and Jack had two.

"The honor's all yours," Jack said, making a wide flourish. "Go on through the window."

"Look who's back," Chip said as Blaze came trotting around the house. "You'd think he'd at least wait until they came out of the cave."

"How do you know he didn't?" Eddie said. "Could be Pop and Lewis are heading for home right now."

They returned to the big oak tree, with Blaze tagging along. There was no sign of Lewis or Mr. Rowans coming back from the cave.

"You know," Chip said, "I've got a better idea than going into Lewis' room."

"Come off it," Jack said, with a wave of the hand. "You're backing out."

"Why, you yourself said all his stuff was burned up. So what's the sense—"

"Talk about reneging," Jack persisted.

"Look, Jack," Chip protested, "it's just that I've got a lot better idea. Give me a chance to tell it, for crying out loud!"

"Am I stopping him, Eddie? And I know *you're* not."

"Maybe we ought to stop him," Eddie said and laughed.

Chip told them that by slipping notes under Lewis' locked door they could get the man worried. Finally, Lewis would get so nervous he would give himself away.

"One note could say," Chip elaborated, " 'You'll never make it alive.' Or one could have something like, 'You thought you could get away with it, didn't you?' "

"Shakespeare's got nothing on him," Eddie said to Jack.

"That's how you'd sign those notes—'William Shakespeare'?" Jack asked.

"Oh, you two are funny," Chip said. "Very funny. Of course, those notes wouldn't be signed."

"They wouldn't have to be," Jack said.

"Oh, no?" Chip said.

"Well, Chip, just think. Just use your head. Who's Lewis going to suspect? Not Blaze. The hound can't write. And he'd hardly suspect Mr. Rowans, who's got a job guiding him around the cave."

"Well, yeah," Chip admitted grudgingly. "But if it wasn't for that, it would be a good idea."

"Sure. It's a good idea, except for all the things that are wrong with it."

For something to do, all of them—including Blaze—hiked to Lewis' wrecked plane.

"It's getting rusty," Chip observed.

"You sound surprised," Jack said. "Don't you know rust is oxidation, and that with heat and moisture around oxidation takes place awfully fast?"

"Okay, okay," Chip said. "I'm convinced."

"Wouldn't you think," Jack interrupted, "that the motor would be worth quite a bit?"

They scrambled over the plane for a look at the motor. It was Jack who noticed that the plane's serial number had been chiseled off. He also pointed out that it had been done very recently. Where the chiseling had been done, there wasn't any rust.

"We should have thought of getting that number," Jack said, scratching his head in irritation, "before Lewis had a chance—"

"You think he did that to keep people from finding out who he really is?" Chip asked.

"Of course," Jack said. "Why, there's a record of all those numbers. All you've got to do is send the number to the aviation commission—or whatever it is." Jack nodded his head thoughtfully as he added, "That guy sure has got something to hide. And that means we get clobbered—but good—if he catches us checking on him."

When they returned home they didn't see Lewis. But Mr. Rowans was talking to someone in the parlor. The stranger had a crew cut, even though he was far from young. His yellowish-brown complexion set off the gray of his hair. He was slight and not over five-feet-five.

After Mr. Rowans had introduced them to the man, he added that Mr. Voxanne was a spelunker and would be renting a room for a while.

"Call me Chuck," Mr. Voxanne said with a smile as he shook hands with Eddie, Jack, and Chip.

As soon as he had the chance, Chip whispered to Jack and Eddie to go with him upstairs.

While they were still on the stairs, Jack asked, "What've you dreamed up now?"

"Don't rush me," Chip answered.

He wouldn't say more than that, until they had reached their room and closed the door after them.

10   *Chip Makes His Move*

"All right, we're here," Jack said. "What's with you?"

Chip stood with his back to the door he had just closed. "All I wanted to know," he said hesitantly, "is what you think of Voxanne?"

"What?" Jack exclaimed dumbfounded. "You got us up here for *that?*"

"You know what I thought, Jack?" Eddie said. "I thought he'd picked up something on Lewis."

"Matter of fact," Jack said, "that's what I thought."

Jack threw himself across his bed, arms spread wide. Eddie walked over to Chip.

"I'll tell you what *I* think of Voxanne," Eddie said.

"You wouldn't catch Lewis or that Beestrom asking you to call them by their first names. I think Chuck Voxanne's okay. I like him."

"That goes for me, too," Jack said from his sprawled position on the bed. Then he sat up quickly. "You think Voxanne and Lewis are—are partners or something, Chip? Is that what you're thinking?"

"All I wanted to know," Chip insisted, "is what you two guys thought of him."

"I don't believe you," Jack said.

"You know something, Jack?" Eddie went over to the bed where Jack was sitting. "For some reason, your brother doesn't want us to like Voxanne." He turned and looked at Chip. "Am I right?"

"Why wouldn't I want you to like him?" Chip asked.

Eddie shrugged. "You tell me."

Jack stood up. "You know," he said, "that's an interesting idea. I mean, Voxanne and Lewis being partners. But what reason have we got for thinking they are?" And after a moment's pause, he asked, "What have *you* got against Voxanne, Chip? Why don't you tell us?"

Both Eddie and Jack stood confronting Chip.

"Don't look at me that way," Chip complained, squirming. "I feel as if you've got me backed to the wall."

"Well, give," Eddie said. "Tell us what you really got us up here for."

Chip took a deep breath, then let it out slowly. It was plain he was trying to decide whether or not to reveal what he was thinking.

Jack suddenly raised both his hands. "Okay, okay," he said, shaking his hands in a gesture of surrender and indifference. "Don't tell us!"

Jack and Eddie went down the stairs then, and Chip followed them dejectedly. He appeared an outcast. But he cheered up considerably when he reached the kitchen and heard Mr. Rowans telling Jack and Eddie that Mr. Beestrom had come back and had rented a room.

"What are you suddenly so happy about?" Jack snapped at his brother.

"Who's happy?" Chip asked, grinning happily. "How about my peeling some of those potatoes, Mr. Rowans?"

"Thank you, Chip," Mr. Rowans said. "Oh," he put

down the potato he was peeling, "I almost forgot." He wiped his hands quickly on a dish towel. "I've got a letter here"—he dug into his hip pocket—"from your father."

As Chip hurriedly clawed open the envelope, Jack waited impatiently. And while Chip read the short letter, Jack read it over Chip's shoulder.

"That's not very good news," Chip said, as he put the single sheet of paper back in the envelope.

"Something wrong?" Mr. Rowans asked.

"Not exactly," Jack answered. "Dad's just being held up. He hasn't been able to get any decent cave pictures —pictures that are unusual or exciting."

"Sorry to hear it," Mr. Rowans said.

"Dad wants us to be patient," Jack added. "Says he'll be back here as soon as he can."

Jack and Chip pitched in and helped Mr. Rowans cook the pot-roast-and-potato supper. He needed the help, too, because the extra guests meant that there was more food to be prepared and served.

Lewis ate hurriedly, not saying a word. Then, without even excusing himself, he went to his room. After the table had been cleared and the dishes done, the

others sat around in the parlor reading or looking at television. Beestrom, sitting at one end of the sofa, kept nodding. His head drooped, and though he struggled to keep awake it appeared to be a losing battle.

Voxanne put his magazine down. "When do you think you'll be getting your cave open?" he asked Eddie's father.

"When?" Mr. Rowans said, turning from the TV western.

"In town," Voxanne said, "there seems to be a lot of talk about something being wrong. In the drugstore I overheard a customer saying there's a bottomless hole you've got to do something about. The druggist disagreed—said a cloudburst had flooded the cave."

Mr. Rowans moved uncomfortably in his armchair. His yellow suspenders were bright against his clean blue shirt. He stroked first one side of his moustache, then the other. "There's still work I've got to do," he answered cryptically.

Chip excused himself first, and Jack and Eddie followed soon afterward.

When they were all in bed, Jack said, "Maybe since Dad's not going to show up for a while we'll have enough time to figure out this mystery about Lewis."

"At the rate we've been going," Eddie said as though half asleep, "it's going to take years."

"What was all that about, Chip?" Jack asked. "Our liking Voxanne or not?"

There was no answer from Chip.

Jack got up on an elbow and looked over toward Chip's bed. The moonlight revealed Chip lying on his side, his face to the wall. "He's asleep already," Jack muttered to himself.

There was a long silence. Finally Jack spoke Eddie's name. There was no answer from Eddie, either. Jack stretched, yawned, and soon he was asleep, too.

Jack woke completely, but not with a start. He soon realized that in addition to the moonlight there was other light in the room. He sat up in bed quickly.

The desk lamp was on. Chip, in his pajamas, stood at the desk. He was bent over, as though he were jotting something down.

"Hey!" Jack whispered loudly. And when Chip turned, he asked, "Have you flipped? What're you doing, anyway?"

"Shhh. You want to wake Eddie?"

Jack got out of bed and rushed over to Chip. He had suddenly guessed what Chip was up to.

"Aw, now," he said, "don't tell me you're writing a note to Lewis."

He looked down at what Chip had printed in big capital letters: WHAT MAKES YOU THINK YOU CAN GET AWAY. . . . Chip finished what he had been writing, by adding . . . WITH YOUR CRIME.

"Every day," Chip said, "I'll slip him a different note. On this order, though."

"Why, that's against the law, isn't it? Besides, he'll know you did it. And you have no proof that there *is* a crime."

"What's going on!" Eddie called from his bed.

"You see," Chip said. "You woke Eddie."

"You know what he's doing, Eddie?" Jack said, striding over to Eddie's bed. "Remember those anonymous letters he told us about, that he was going to write to Lewis? He just wrote one."

Eddie sat up in bed. "I thought you decided—"

"Of course," Chip broke in. "I wasn't going to write them when we were the only ones around for him to suspect. But Voxanne's here now and—"

"You mean that?" Jack exploded. "You'd let Voxanne take the blame?"

"No!" Chip protested. "I like the guy, too. That's why I asked you if you did. And when you said you did, I decided to call the whole thing off."

"Yeah," Jack said. "Go on. You'd better make it good."

"But then Beestrom came back. And with him here Lewis will be all confused. He won't be sure who's writing the notes. You get it?"

"Isn't this breaking the law?" Jack asked, appealing to Eddie, who had finally gotten out of bed. "I think it's a crazy idea."

"Jack!" Eddie exclaimed, pushing by him. "Chip's going!"

Jack spun around. But his brother was no longer in the room.

11 *A Puzzling Reaction*

Jack and Eddie rushed out the door and down the hall, which was lit dimly by a night-light. But they stopped abruptly before they reached the door to Lewis' room. Chip was nowhere in sight!

"What happened to him?" Eddie asked.

"I don't know," Jack whispered back. "Golly. It's—it's like he's vanished into thin air!"

Eddie and Jack moved quickly up to Lewis' door.

"If Lewis caught him slipping that note under the door. . . ." Jack whispered his thought aloud.

"But Chip didn't have time to slip a note under the door. We made it here in two seconds flat—you know that he couldn't have delivered that note."

The old farmhouse creaked in the darkness. The eerie sounds intensified the silence, made it seem ominous.

"Chip!" Jack called for his brother in a loud whisper. "Chip!"

They waited silently for an answer, but there was no sound but the creaking of the old house.

Eddie looked uneasily over his shoulder. "Maybe he went downstairs."

"But I don't see why he'd do that," Jack said.

"I don't, either."

Nevertheless, they tiptoed down the steps and through the moonlit rooms.

"He's not down here," Jack said for the fifth time.

"Don't get excited," Eddie told him.

"I'm not excited. I'm beginning to get worried, though. That's for sure."

"I don't want to wake Pop yet," Eddie said. "Or call the cops."

"Oh, no!"

"But, Jack, what should we do? We've got to do something."

"Let's take another look upstairs. Maybe he's under

the hall rug." Jack laughed, but it was as though he were trying to still his fears. "Come on!"

They found the hall as empty as it had been before.

"Maybe he's back in our room," Jack said anxiously. "Maybe he never left. Maybe we've just imagined the whole thing."

As soon as they stepped through the door, Chip sat up in bed. "Where've you guys been? I've been waiting for you—" His laughter broke into what he was saying, but he still managed to add, "What a neat trick I pulled on you guys!"

Jack rushed across the moonlit room, grabbed his brother, and started dragging him out of bed. Chip protested but continued laughing, unable to stop.

"Okay!" Jack was too relieved to be truly angry. "Where've you been, buddy?"

Chip explained that since they had come rushing out after him, instead of heading for Lewis' door he had gone in the other direction down the hall. When he had seen them go downstairs, he had quickly gone to Lewis' door and slipped the note under it. Then he had come back to their room and jumped into bed.

"What should we do to him?" Eddie asked Jack.

"Don't you know, Chip, that you had us worried?"

"It might work at that," Jack said. "The note, I mean. It just might get us some action."

"I thought you said it was against the law," Eddie reminded Jack, "to scare people with notes."

"I never said that," Jack objected. "I just *wondered* if it was illegal. Maybe it won't be necessary to write a lot of those notes, Chip. Maybe just one will do the trick."

"You mean we'll know tomorrow morning?" Chip asked. "When we see Lewis, and see how that note hit him?"

"Hmmm." Jack nodded. "Could be. Could be we'll know something tomorrow morning."

"It'll be at breakfast," Chip said. "You think Lewis might play it cool and act as if he never got the note?"

"How should I know?" Jack answered. "What do you say we just wait and see what happens?"

But Chip kept asking questions after they got in bed. It was late by the time they all fell asleep, and so the next morning they overslept. Worried that they had missed Lewis, they raced frantically getting dressed.

Jack, Chip, and Eddie came into the kitchen at the

same time. All three of them looked as if they had been running.

"Is Lewis gone, Pop?" Eddie asked.

Mr. Rowans had eggs in a red mixing bowl. He was beating them with a fork. "Thought you fellows were never coming down for breakfast," he said. "Lewis hasn't come down, either. Eddie, how about it? Would you pump some water?"

Eddie went to the hand pump near the kitchen sink. It drew water from the cistern into a tank near the pump.

"One good thing about that cloudburst," Mr. Rowans said, "it sure filled our cistern. Something good in the worst of things, I guess."

"Is the mud in the cave drying up?" Chip asked.

"Never enough mud to cause me any trouble," Mr. Rowans told Chip. "My trouble is all those strange sounds. How to exorcise 'em, get rid of 'em."

"Did you hear them again yesterday?" Chip asked.

Mr. Rowans put butter in a big cast iron skillet. He nodded. "Every bit as bad," he said, "if not worse. I just can't believe they're ghosts. I'm an adult. Grown men don't believe in ghosts. . . . You sit down, boys.

These eggs will be for you."

"How about Lewis?" Eddie asked. "When's he having breakfast?"

Mr. Rowans stopped stirring the eggs. He looked from Eddie to Jack to Chip. "You want Lewis for something?" he asked suspiciously.

"No, Pop, no," Eddie said emphatically. "What would we want him for?"

"It's just funny he isn't here," Chip said. "Golly, how late is it, anyhow?"

"Sit down, Chip," Jack said. "Mr. Rowans wants us to get going on our breakfast."

"I'm mighty thankful to Mr. Lewis," Eddie's father said. "Now that I can't open the cave, I need that guide money he's paying me."

While Eddie and the Power boys ate, they nervously kept an eye on the door through which Lewis would come. Mr. Rowans noticed this. He had just started to ask them what was wrong when Lewis came sailing through the door.

"Morning," he mumbled, as he went straight to the table and sat down.

Eddie and the boys couldn't help but watch him.

They wanted some indication of what the note had meant to him.

Their silent scrutiny began to bother him. The movement of his knife slowed as he stropped butter on a whole slice of bread. "Yeah?" he challenged them. His hair was wet-combed and sleek. His dark eyes moved from one face to another even more rapidly than usual. "Anything wrong?" He glanced down at his chest. "I got a shirt on. I thought maybe I came down in my pajamas, the way you were staring at me. . . . Well, what is it that's bothering you?"

12 *Eddie Spills the Beans*

Jack, Chip, and Eddie glanced at one another for help.

"Oh, uh—uh—" Chip stammered. "What's that on your bread, Mr. Lewis? I thought I saw a speck—or—something in the butter."

Lewis looked down at the slice of bread that still lay flat on the palm of his hand. He scraped and explored the heavily spread butter with his knife. "This butter's okay," he said. "I don't see anything in it."

"My brother's dizzy," Jack said and laughed. "He's seeing spots in front of his eyes again."

A suggestion of a smile came into Lewis' restless, piercing eyes. He took a bite of the bread.

"What do you say, Jack?" Eddie was grinning widely to make light of the whole situation—just as Jack had been doing. "Will you help me take Chip out for some fresh air?"

"Wait a second." Chip hurried to finish the food on his plate. "I do need the air." He was playing along with their gag. "I feel kind of—you know. . . ."

As soon as they had excused themselves, Jack and Eddie hustled Chip away from the house. Blaze rose lazily from a shady spot and walked toward them. At a safe distance they stopped, and Jack accused Chip of having gotten them into a tight spot.

"Me?" Chip asked in angry disbelief. "You guys were staring at Lewis as much as I was."

"Who's talking about that?" Jack demanded. "I'm talking about that kookie note you shoved under his door."

"Why, you thought it was a good idea," Chip objected. "Now you're saying—"

"Okay, so I changed my mind," Jack said.

"I never did go for the idea," Eddie said, shaking his head.

"You guys," Chip said with disgust. "What pals!"

"Well, look, Chip," Jack said, "you see what that note's accomplishing?"

"No, I don't," Chip said. "I haven't seen anything. Have you, Eddie?"

"As far as I can see, it's just made him more touchy than ever," Eddie replied. "It's putting more pressure on him, so he'll just hurry faster than ever to finish whatever he's doing here."

"How'd you figure all that out," Chip asked, "just from watching him butter a piece of bread?"

"Knock it off," Jack warned them under his breath as he looked toward the house. "Here they come. . . ."

Mr. Rowans smiled as he and Lewis approached the boys. It was clear that they were going to the cave, for they wore coveralls and hard hats.

"Looks like you're plotting something mighty bad," Mr. Rowans said.

He stopped to tell Eddie that Beestrom had already eaten and had left the house. Voxanne still hadn't had his breakfast, and Mr. Rowans asked Eddie to fix it for him.

"Will do, Pop," Eddie said.

Mr. Rowans hurried off, for Lewis hadn't waited for

him but had walked on impatiently. Blaze trotted after them.

Voxanne was standing in the kitchen, drinking coffee from a mug, when the boys returned to the house. He had on a hard green hat. The copper buttons of the new denim coat he was wearing shone brightly.

"I'll make your breakfast right away, Mr. Voxanne," Eddie said. "I'm supposed to."

Voxanne shook his head. "No, no, no," he said. "This coffee'll do me fine. But here's what I *would* like. First, call me Chuck, not Mr. Voxanne . . . remember? And I'd like a sandwich or two to take along for my lunch. I'm making a day of it, you see. I'm assuming I'll eventually get hungry."

While Eddie made the sandwiches, Voxanne told him that he had wanted to go exploring caves with Eddie's father and Lewis, but Lewis hadn't wanted company.

"You're not going alone, are you, Chuck?" Chip asked.

"If I'd gone with Lewis, it would have been the same as if I'd been alone. What's he so jittery about? Do you know?"

"We know he's looking for something," Chip answered, "and can't find it."

"Oh, yeah?" Voxanne said.

"There's an engraved penny mixed up in it, too, and—"

Chip stopped. Jack, standing behind Voxanne, was glowering at his brother and shaking his head.

Eddie, who didn't notice Jack's silent warning, said, "It's pretty confusing to start with the penny. We'd better start from the beginning." He began to give an account of the plane crash. He related how they had found a penny with a mysterious engraving on it, and how they had given it to Lewis when he claimed that he had lost it. He even mentioned the spooky noises in the cave, which Lewis might be making so that he could have the cave all to himself and have a better chance of finding whatever it was he was looking for.

Jack kept on trying to give Eddie the high sign, but without any luck.

"We put a note under Lewis' door last night," Eddie said, still intent on the story he was telling. "It was Chip's idea." And in mentioning Chip, he glanced toward him. That was when he saw the stern expression on Chip's face and realized that Chip was shaking his head as unobtrusively as possible. He glanced at Jack and saw that the older Power boy was doing the same thing.

Voxanne couldn't help but notice what was going on. He grinned as he put his coffee mug on the table.

"All right," he said, "you don't have to tell me about the note if you don't want to. But I have a pretty good idea what it was like. I know the sort of notes red-blooded American boys write. You must have aimed to put a lot of fear in him." Voxanne laughed. "Good for you, fellows."

The instant Voxanne left, Eddie asked, "What was all that head-shaking about?"

"You mean you don't know?" Jack said.

"Jack's worried—" Chip began.

"You're darned right I'm worried," Jack interrupted his brother. "Why did you two guys have to sound off? We don't know anything about Voxanne."

"He seems like a nice guy," Eddie said.

"Yeah *seems* like a nice guy," Jack snapped. "Why? Because he wants us to call him Chuck? For all we know—"

"You're not back to that idea again, are you?"

"Yeah, Eddie," Jack said. "Yeah, I am—if you mean that Voxanne and Lewis might be in cahoots."

"But how about what Voxanne said?" Chip asked. "He said Lewis didn't want him to go along in the cave. And if they're pals—"

"*He* said that."

"You mean he was lying?" Chip asked.

"Right!" Jack exclaimed, stabbing a forefinger at Chip as though he had just asked a prize question. "Right! He might be lying. You catch on fast."

Eddie rushed across the kitchen. "We'd better get going." He took a hard hat from a hook on the wall. "If Voxanne tells Lewis we're the ones who slipped him the note, we're going to get a clobbering."

"So where are you running?" Chip asked.

"If we stick close to Lewis, we'll know whether Voxanne tells him or not. Then we'll know for sure what kind of a guy Voxanne is."

In the immensity of the cave, they didn't come across either Voxanne or Lewis. But in the course of searching for them, they came to a foot-wide crevice, well off the tourist path laid out by Mr. Rowans.

Chip straddled the crevice. With the beam of his flashlight he explored its depths.

Both Jack and Eddie stepped completely over the deep crack.

"Any water down there?" Jack asked.

"Come here!" Chip said excitedly.

"Chuck Voxanne's not down there," Eddie said. "Don't try to tell me that."

"They're bones!" Chip exclaimed. "I'm sure that they're bones!"

Jack and Eddie stood at the edge of the crevice and stared down into it. They all aimed their flashlights directly at what was unquestionably a pathetic huddle of bones.

"You see the skull?" Chip asked excitedly. "It's a skull, isn't it? You think this might be from that vanished race that—"

"It's an Indian skull," Eddie said.

"Really!" Chip exclaimed. "How do you know?"

"Right on top of the skull," Eddie said. "Do you see that kind of greenish color? That's caused by Indian jewelry. It always leaves that greenish kind of mark."

"I'd like to get down in there and look around," Chip said. "What is it—ten feet deep? It's certainly not more than fifteen."

"Just the same," Jack told his brother, "you'd need a steel cable ladder—or a rope ladder."

"You think I'd let you guys go down there?" Eddie said with vehemence. "I wouldn't let you even if you had a—a—an air-conditioned elevator. That stuff could be scientifically important. And if people go messing it up, that would just confuse the scientists."

"Right," Jack agreed, nodding his head sagely.

"For one thing," Eddie pointed out, "it would throw them off as far as dating the bones."

"Are they important, Eddie?" Chip asked. "You act as if they are. You think they're the ones Beestrom's looking for? I mean, that vanished race?"

Jack continued to look down at the bones as he said, "You know that spirit we heard? 'Don't shoot,' and all that jazz. Maybe it once belonged to that skeleton."

"We ought to tell Beestrom, don't you think?" Chip asked.

"Why not?" Eddie said. "If those bones are real hot stuff, they might give Pop just the publicity he needs.

You know, Pop has sunk all his money in this cave, fixing it up. What's more, it's money he made the hard way—farming. He's just got to get a break. But we can't tell him about this and get his hopes up. First we've got to find out from Beestrom if these bones rate publicity."

"Well, this should be better than Chip's white bats," Jack said.

"The ones that don't exist, you mean?" Eddie said. "I agree with you there."

Chip ignored their words. "What I want to know," he said, "is whether we'll be able to find this part of the cave again."

Eddie assured Chip that he had been at the crevice before—though he had never noticed the bones—and knew exactly how to reach it.

"But there's one thing we're forgetting," Eddie said. "If Lewis gets to us before we get to Beestrom—"

"Yeah, yeah," Jack interrupted. "I know what you mean."

"Well, if we've made a great discovery," Chip said with urgency, "we just have to get to Beestrom. I sure wish I had my camera with me. Some shots of those bones might be just what Dad needs for his cave story."

As soon as they arrived home, they hid in the hayloft of the dilapidated barn. Lying in a bed of hay, they could see every approach to the farmhouse through the cracks in the walls. They saw Mr. Rowans return alone, but, though they waited until it began to get dark, Beestrom, Voxanne, and Lewis did not show up. And it was Beestrom they were eager to see.

Before going into the house they stood in a huddle under the big oak tree near the kitchen door deciding what to do.

"Maybe Beestrom got home before we went up in that old barn," Chip said.

"And don't forget Lewis could be in there, too," Eddie pointed out. "He wouldn't bother Pop. It's just us he'd be laying for."

Chip whistled for Blaze, explaining that they could at least take him in for some protection.

They entered the lighted kitchen slowly, warily. When they heard movement in the cellar, Eddie opened the cellar door and called down, "Is that you, Pop?"

Mr. Rowans started up the stairs. He carried a coil of electric wire. Instead of answering Eddie's question, he said, "Here's some wire I plumb forgot I had. That narrow cutoff just after you get in the cave—that's where I'll be able to use it."

"Where's Mr. Lewis, Pop?" Eddie asked as casually as he could. "Where *is* everybody, anyhow?"

Mr. Rowans put the coil of wire on the kitchen floor, leaning it against the wall. After straightening he remained thoughtfully silent for a moment. "You haven't got yourself in trouble with Mr. Lewis, have you?" he asked, looking from one to another of the three boys.

They all acted amazed that he should even ask such a question.

"Well," Mr. Rowans said, "I'm glad to hear you're not tangling with him. He's not one to get involved with. You know, boys, there's no better way to get to know what a man's really like than to be with him underground for a few days."

"What's he been up to, Pop?" Eddie asked.

Mr. Rowans shrugged.

"Does he just get on your nerves?"

"Yeah, Eddie." Mr. Rowans nodded. "That's it."

Throughout supper they expected Lewis and Voxanne to arrive at any minute. But neither man appeared, nor did Beestrom. The boys sat around for a long time afterward, uncomfortably aware of the lateness of the hour. Finally Mr. Rowans went up to bed and advised them to do the same.

Upstairs in their bedroom they stood around anxiously.

"I bet Beestrom would be here," Chip said, "if he knew the news we had for him."

"Lewis and Voxanne are always here by this time, aren't they?" Jack asked.

"Up to tonight, they have been," Eddie admitted.

"There's only one thing it can mean." Jack snatched a pillow from the bed, held it with one hand, and punched it with the other. "They're figuring out a surefire way to clobber us."

"What're we going to do?" Chip asked. "Stay up all night?"

Jack tossed the pillow onto the bed. He ran his fingers through his red hair. "I'd rather be wide-awake when they show up, wouldn't you?"

"Staying up isn't going to make me wide-awake," Chip said as he started to skin out of his T-shirt. "I'll just get sleepier than I already am." He started to take off his trousers, then changed his mind.

"The guy's decided to sleep with his pants on," Jack said.

"Jack, will you give me a chance to say something?" Chip asked.

Jack shrugged. "Yeah. Sure. Go ahead."

"What if something happens to us? If Lewis— Now wait, Jack, let me finish. I think what we've got to do is leave a message for Beestrom about those bones. Golly, if they're important we have to do it."

"Maybe Chip's right—for once," Jack said to Eddie.

"I could draw a map," Eddie said. "That'd be easy enough to do. With the map, Beestrom ought to be able to go right to all that stuff."

Eddie busied himself at once with the map. Jack and Chip watched as he indicated the exact location of the bones. Eddie added a few words explaining how they had discovered the bones and wanted him to know about them.

"What'll I do," Chip said when Eddie finished, "just slip it under Beestrom's door?"

"You're going to become an expert note-slipper," Jack said. "First that note for Lewis, and now this."

"Well, it was my idea," Chip said, "giving Beestrom this dope. So I guess I ought to deliver it."

The hall was dimly lit, just as it had been the night Chip slipped the note under Lewis' door.

Chip strode forward on tiptoe. He was only a few steps from Lewis' room, when the bathroom door farther down the hall burst open.

Chip was so startled that he couldn't move. He simply stood where he was and stared at Lewis, who was wearing bedroom slippers and a bathrobe.

Finally Chip became aware of the paper in his hand. In the same instant, he was certain that Lewis would mistake it for another warning note intended for him.

As Chip turned and ran, he had the feeling that Lewis had started after him and was closing the gap between them! Lewis would grab him before he reached the room where Jack and Eddie were waiting!

14   *Delayed Delivery*

Chip jerked the door open. He scrambled into the room, closed the door, and locked it as fast as he could.

When he turned, his back still against the door, Jack and Eddie rushed up to him.

"Lewis!" Chip panted. "He's out there!" It was all the explanation he could manage.

"What'd he do?" Jack whispered. "Chase you?"

Chip nodded, still breathing hard.

"But he's not trying to come in here after you," Eddie said, puzzled.

Chip wanted a few moments to catch his breath. Then he told them what had happened in the hall.

"Where's Lewis now?" Jack asked. "Are you sure, Chip, you didn't imagine it all?"

"Oh, yeah," Chip answered sarcastically. "I imagined it all. Sure."

"Well, if you didn't," Jack demanded, "where *is* he?"

"How would I know?" Chip snapped. "Maybe he wanted to get to bed. He was in his bathrobe. If—if you don't believe he's in the house, why don't you go on out and see?"

"It just seems funny—"

"It wasn't funny," Chip broke in on Jack. "That feeling he was going to grab me stayed right with me. Oh, did it ever!"

Jack must finally have been convinced. Though he had seen Chip lock the door, he propped a chair under its knob. "No point," he said, "trying again tonight— I mean, to get Eddie's map to Beestrom."

The bright morning sunlight helped to awaken them. But Beestrom and Lewis, quarreling out in the hall, completed the job. There was no mistaking Beestrom's exaggeratedly cultured manner of speaking or Lewis' unfriendly tones.

Eddie, Jack, and Chip sat up in bed.

"It's Beestrom out there," Chip said, surprised.

Jack held up his hand to silence him and they all listened intently. At one point, Jack moved silently from his bed and put his ear to the door. The voices gradually became fainter as the men went downstairs.

"Did you hear them?" Jack asked as he came away from the door. "Those two guys must be partners. Did you hear Lewis when he told Beestrom he didn't want more of his help?"

"And didn't he say something about not wanting to see Beestrom anymore?" Eddie asked.

Jack nodded and said, "You remember the night Beestrom showed up? I'm used to him now. But that night he sure looked like pure, unadulterated Frankenstein. I—I just never have been able to see him as a respectable scientist."

"What are we going to do with Eddie's map now?" Chip asked.

Jack shrugged. "We're not giving it to Beestrom. That's for sure. He's a phony!"

"What if I'd put it under his door last night?" Chip said. "That would've been a laugh."

"You know what this means, guys?" Eddie said. "It's not just Lewis and Voxanne that we have to watch out for. There'll be Beestrom, too. It's going to be—"

A knock sounded on their door.

"Who do you think it is?" Chip whispered.

Jack shrugged.

"Anybody awake in there?" a voice on the other side of the door asked.

"Voxanne!" Jack and Chip whispered simultaneously.

Eddie nodded. "Yeah. What—what are we going to do?"

"Lewis might be with him!" Jack whispered, his eyes wide.

"We've got to answer the door," Chip whispered.

Before either Jack or Eddie could stop him, Chip moved quickly to the door and opened it.

Chuck Voxanne smiled as he walked into the bedroom. He looked as if he had just shaved. A towel hung over his shoulder. Each gray hair of his crew cut stood at attention.

"I see you're not dressed yet," Voxanne said. "But at least I didn't wake you."

The three boys stood speechless. They had been thinking of him as a possible enemy, and his continued friendliness came as a shock.

"I wouldn't have barged in on you so early," Voxanne said, "but I wanted to report to you on Lewis. He hasn't found what he's looking for. And that note of yours, fellows, has got him searching harder than ever. He was up mighty late last night. That meant I was, too, keeping tabs on him."

"Maybe we ought to write another note," Chip said. "What do you think?"

Voxanne rubbed his chin thoughtfully with the end of the towel. "Not just yet," he said. "For now, I think we ought to watch him. And remember, any time I can help you—I'm ready."

After Voxanne left, the boys looked at each other sheepishly.

"That's why Lewis didn't grab me last night," Chip said. "He didn't know for sure we'd written the note. Voxanne hadn't told him."

"Why'd he chase you then?" Jack asked. "You said he chased you."

Chip smiled sheepishly. "Maybe he didn't," he said.

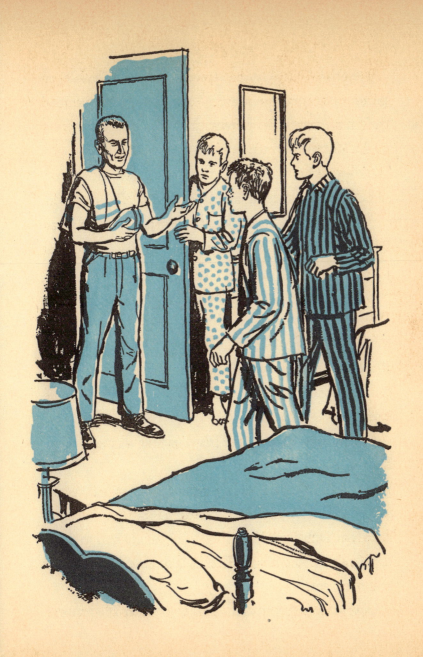

"I never did turn around to see. And since I was expecting him to chase me. . . ."

"And now we know why they got home so late last night," Eddie pointed out. "Beestrom and Lewis were searching like mad—because of our note. And Voxanne was busy keeping an eye on them."

"You think Chuck's okay, huh?" Jack asked, somewhat dubiously.

"Don't you?" Eddie countered.

Jack shrugged. "Yeah," he said. "I guess so."

After breakfast, the Power boys and Eddie took up their position again in the old barn. This time they had Blaze with them. They waited and waited, but Lewis didn't appear. This only increased their eagerness to spy on him.

"He's late getting started because he was up so late last night," Eddie commented.

When Lewis finally showed up, Mr. Rowans wasn't with him. They followed Lewis, keeping a considerable distance behind him. Chip continually had to order Blaze not to run ahead of them, so that he wouldn't give them away.

Lewis stopped a few times as if to study the ground.

"He must be looking for a new cave opening," Eddie said. "Watch the way he's poking around. I don't know what else he'd be looking for."

At the foot of the slope a jumble of slablike rocks slanted in every direction. Ahead of them on a plateau —broken here and there by rocky outthrusts—Lewis continued to explore the ground.

Eddie had brought hotdogs in a brown paper bag. They discussed building a fire on one of the rocks that was fairly level and roasting the hotdogs, but Jack didn't like the idea. He insisted that the smoke of their fire would be noticed by Lewis.

Blaze, stretched out on one of the rocks, suddenly growled. He rose slowly, angry and tensed for attack.

Chip seized the dog's collar. "I don't see anything, Blaze boy. What're you growling about?"

Jack grabbed Chip's arm to silence him. The three boys stood motionless, listening. A strange rising and falling sound seemed to be coming from under the rock on which they were sitting.

As Blaze's growl turned to barking, Chip bent down and started scolding the Dalmatian. "You don't want Lewis to know we're here, do you?" he asked.

"Say," Jack said with sudden realization, "Lewis can't be making those noises. He just came into sight again, away off in front of us."

"Talking about finding new caves," Eddie said, pursuing his own thought, "this might be a new one, you know. Maybe the one Lewis is looking for! Or it could be just another entrance to Pop's cave."

The sounds faded to a whisper and then stopped altogether.

Blaze looked about alertly.

"They stopped," Chip said.

"Since Lewis didn't make those strange sounds we just heard," Jack said, "he probably didn't make all the others either."

"Yeah," Chip said, prodding his brother. "Go on."

"Do I have to?" Jack asked. "Can't you draw your own conclusion?"

"You don't mean that a ghost is making them? Maybe the ghost of those bones? Or—or the ghost who asked Jesse James not to shoot?"

"I don't know whether they're noises made by spirits or not. All I know is this. The way it looks from all these weird goings-on, Eddie's dad's going to have a heck of a long wait before he can open up his cave to paying customers. It's going to be real tough for him—"

"Look who's coming," Chip said.

Jack and Eddie turned and looked up the stone-littered slope.

15 *Caves and Coins*

"How're you, fellows?" Chuck Voxanne greeted the boys as he came toward them. He was wearing a green hard hat. His coveralls were muddy. The thick rubber pads on his knees looked like grotesque calluses.

"You look as if you've been doing some cave crawling, Chuck," Eddie said with a grin.

Voxanne nodded. "And I've also been keeping an eye on Lewis. I see you're watching him, too."

"We just discovered something," Chip said. "Maybe it's what he's looking for."

"Oh, yes?" Voxanne said with great interest.

Eagerly they told Voxanne about the strange sounds

coming from under the rock. He was interested, but not excited.

"Probably made by drafts of air inside a cave," he said. "It happens often."

"I hope that's all they are," Eddie said. "Drafts. Nothing more than that."

"Would you stay here and listen to these?" Jack asked. "They might come again. Can you tell the kind of sounds made by drafts?"

Voxanne and the boys began moving the rocks in hopes that they could find an opening. Suddenly the sounds began again. They all stopped what they were doing to listen.

"Sure," Voxanne said at once. "They're caused by a draft, all right. Not unusual—not at all."

"Man, am I glad to hear that!" Eddie exclaimed delightedly. "Pop's probably been worrying about nothing all along, and—"

"Wait a minute, Eddie," Jack interrupted. "Those weren't just sounds we heard before, you know. They were words."

"Oh, yeah," Eddie said disappointedly.

"No draft's going to say, 'Don't shoot!' " Chip added.

"Right," Eddie said. "Of course. I don't know how I could've forgotten about that. Probably because I wanted to."

They continued to move the rocks, and gradually they uncovered a ragged opening in the ground. Finally, only one extremely heavy rock barred their entrance into the cave. With all of them trying to lift it, they still could hardly budge it. Each time they lifted it an inch, Chip hurriedly shoved small rocks under the big one to keep the gain they had made. At last there was a hole large enough for them to crawl through. They all lit the carbide lamps clipped to their hard hats.

"I'll lead the way," Voxanne volunteered, kneeling at the small opening to the cave.

But before he started, Chip asked, "What're we going to do about Blaze?"

Voxanne stood up. "Might be a good idea," he said, "to let him lead the way."

The boys explained that they had never been able to get Blaze to go into a cave.

"But the thing is," Jack said, "can we afford to leave him out here? Lewis will have a lot better chance of spotting this opening we made."

With his lips tightly compressed, Voxanne nodded thoughtfully. Then he looked off in the distance. "Where is Lewis? I don't see him. Maybe he's moved on."

"Anyhow, Jack," Eddie said, "maybe Blaze'll follow us in this time. You and Chip both are always saying you can't predict what that hound's liable to do."

Voxanne knelt down at the cave opening again.

"Wish I had those kneepads of yours," Chip said.

Voxanne turned his head to look up at them. "It might not be too long a crawl. I'll take it slow. You fellows really ought to get yourselves some kneepads."

The narrow tunnel through which they crawled turned out to be over thirty feet long. At the other end was a vast room of solid rock. It was a relief to stretch and walk around after all the crawling they had done.

Chip swept the beam of his flashlight over the walls. A glistening trickle of water dribbled down one side.

"Let me have that a minute," Voxanne said, taking the flashlight from Chip. "I think I saw something interesting."

Voxanne moved to the far wall, with Jack, Chip, and Eddie trailing after him. There was a fissure in the rock wall. Voxanne immediately announced that he wanted to explore it. Getting down on all fours, he started into the fissure.

He had disappeared up to his knees when Chip remarked, "That's sure a tight fit."

"Too tight," Jack said.

Eddie nodded. "It's a tight squeeze, all right."

They stood looking down at Voxanne's legs, waiting for the man to move on the rest of the way into the opening. Their carbide lamps gave a feeble light in the immensity of the rock-walled room.

"I don't think he's going to get anywhere," Eddie said, a suggestion of alarm in his voice. "It looks to me as if that's no more than a crack in the wall."

"He hasn't moved for a long time," Chip said, definitely alarmed.

Eddie quickly got down on his hands and knees. "You all right?" he shouted into the fissure.

The question echoed eerily from the walls. There was no other answer. In the terrible silence that followed, the boys looked at one another. The ghostly light from their lamps accentuated their fright.

"We've got to get him out!" Eddie shouted up at

Jack and Chip, who watched anxiously.

Out—out—out, the walls echoed mockingly.

They tried to be careful as they pulled on Voxanne's legs. At the same time, in order to drag him from the fissure they had to use a great deal of force. Frantically they scrambled about, getting in each other's way in their attempts to free him.

When they had Voxanne all the way out and had turned him over, they were worried by his almost lifeless appearance. "He's not dead, is he?" Chip asked.

"Chip!" Jack snapped nervously. "Can't you see that he passed out? That's all."

"We're not going to be able to get him out of here," Eddie said. "That tunnel's thirty feet long, if it's an inch."

"Yeah," Jack agreed. "Why, look how tough it was just hauling him out of the crack in the wall."

"What're we going to do?" Chip asked.

Eddie didn't answer. First he opened the front of Voxanne's coveralls. Next he unbuttoned his shirt collar and loosened his belt.

"My guess is that carbon dioxide got him," Eddie said. "In a confined space like that, fumes can really knock you out. His lamp alone gave off a lot of CO_2. This isn't the first time it's happened. I've heard of a lot of cases."

"Is he going to be all right, you think?" Chip asked anxiously. "How about some water? Maybe he needs a drink of water."

Eddie spread wide the opening of Voxanne's cover-all. "He'll be okay," he said. "There's nothing else we can do but what we're doing."

"I saw water trickling down the wall," Chip persisted. "I could try to—"

"Look," Eddie said. "He's got a coin in his pocket." The coin was visible through the cloth of Voxanne's shirt pocket.

"You got coins on the brain," Chip said as he rose to his feet. "I'm going to see if I can get some water."

By this time Eddie had taken the coin out of Voxanne's pocket. "Look at this, would you!" he exclaimed. "Another 1864 Indian Head cent!"

Chip forgot about getting water. He knelt down beside Eddie again and said, "Maybe it's Lewis'."

Eddie took his pocket magnifying glass from his trousers.

"If it is, what would Chuck be doing with it?" Jack asked Chip.

"You'd think, too," Chip said, "that if he'd gotten it from Lewis he'd have told us about it."

"This has a different engraving on it!" Eddie exclaimed. In his excitement he jumped to his feet. But he immediately returned to examining the engraving. "Wow! You know what's on this one?"

"What?" Chip asked eagerly.

Eddie studied the engraving.

"Hey!" Jack protested. "Come on. Tell us."

"I just wanted to make sure," Eddie said.

"Make sure?" Chip asked. "Of what?"

"Just calm down, will you?" Eddie said. "Both of you guys. We gotta keep our heads. This penny's got the other half of the bone figure—"

"The other half?" Chip asked, perplexed.

"Yeah," Eddie said. "The other half of what's engraved on the penny that Lewis has."

"That means that he," Chip said, pointing down at Voxanne, "is teamed up with Lewis after all?"

"Chip—" Eddie said.

"And he was playing us for suckers," Chip went

right on angrily. "Trying to—"

"Chip!" Eddie insisted. "Just listen to this! This is the payoff! I understand—"

Voxanne stirred a little.

"Hey, he's coming out of it," Chip whispered.

"What do you understand?" Jack demanded of Eddie.

Eddie put up his hands to silence him. "Wait, Jack! Wait! I'm afraid he might be coming out of it!"

16   *An Unavoidable Conclusion*

Voxanne lay still, however, and after a few moments Eddie went on to say that together the engravings on the two pennies made sense to him. They indicated an odd-shaped area in the cave—a place he recognized.

"Let's go there tonight," Eddie said, keeping his voice down. "I know where it is. We'll be able to lick this mystery—tonight!"

"What's that bone on the two pennies all about?" Jack asked. "Is it what Beestrom thought it was? Has it got anything to do with the bones we found?"

Voxanne moved his head weakly from side to side. The three boys watched him anxiously.

"Come on, Eddie," Jack urged. "Tell us about the pennies before he comes to."

Speaking quickly and keeping his voice low, Eddie explained that he was certain that the engraved bone shape represented two circular cave rooms joined by a corridor. The vertical lines on Voxanne's penny probably stood for a waterfall. The varied objects within the circles could be drawings of stalactites and stalagmites, serving as landmarks, just as Beestrom had suggested earlier.

"I'm sure of all this," Eddie said. "Absolutely. I know that part of the cave better than I know you. I realize just where those two round rooms are—and the corridor between them. If you drew the setup or engraved it, what you'd have would look very much like a bone or a dumbbell."

"What do you think we'll find," Chip asked, "when we go there tonight?"

Voxanne's eyelids fluttered, and Jack held up his hand for silence. "Shhh!" he hissed. When Voxanne started to sit up, Jack and Eddie quickly got down beside him to help him. He came around fast after that. Within a couple of minutes he assured the boys that he was all right and made it to his feet without their help.

"I'm ashamed of myself." He smiled faintly. "Those gases in that crack in the wall sure kayoed me. Guess I'm not the spelunker I thought I was."

That night the boys went up to their bedroom early. They got together all the things they would need for cave exploration, including Chip's camera and other photographic equipment. Then they lay on their beds with their clothes on and the lights off. They were so excited that they didn't even doze.

"What do you say we go?" Chip finally whispered.

"There's no rush," Eddie replied. "We want to be sure everybody's asleep."

"Especially Voxanne," Jack whispered. "But I think it's okay now."

Waiting must have been as hard on Eddie as it was on the others. His bed creaked as he sat up at once. "Let's go," he said, getting to his feet. "But first we've got to leave a note. You just don't go into a cave without letting somebody know or without giving some idea when you expect to be back. We never should have done it yesterday either—even though there were four of us."

Eddie wrote the note fast, scrawling it on a whole sheet of paper.

They didn't turn on their flashlights until after they had sneaked out of their room and tiptoed downstairs. By the time they reached the kitchen they were walking quickly. Eddie left the note on the table.

As soon as they went out of the back door, Chip said querulously, "Where's all that moonlight? Now, when we need it, it's not around."

"The moon's out," Eddie said, looking up. "It's just that there are all those clouds."

A luminous green glow showed through the clouds —fast-moving clouds that seemed intent on obscuring the moon.

"Moonlight's not going to make any difference any-way," Jack said, "once we get down in the cave."

"You won't mind my going along," a voice from the darkness said loudly and clearly.

Startled, all three boys reacted in exactly the same way. They instantly aimed their flashlights at the point in the darkness from which the voice had come. The

three beams converged, spotlighting Chuck Voxanne's face.

Voxanne's smile wasn't weak now, as it had been when he had regained consciousness in the cave. It was wide, self-satisfied. And under his smile the boys saw a gun leveled at them!

"It's a gun, all right," Voxanne said, acknowledging their stares. "I just thought I'd bring it in case you *did* mind my going along with you."

"Why should we mind?" Jack asked.

"Does that gun really work?" Eddie smiled uneasily. "I didn't know you went in for practical jokes."

"This isn't a joke," Voxanne said. "You see, I know all about your plans for tonight. I overheard what you said in the cave."

"You heard?" Chip blurted. "How? You were—"

"No." Voxanne shook his head. "That's what you thought. You *thought* I was unconscious."

"But how about those fumes?" Chip insisted. "Didn't they—"

Chip stopped because Voxanne was shaking his head again. He hadn't been unconscious, he told them smugly, but had merely pretended to be. He had also put his penny where they would be sure to find it because he wanted to hear precisely what he had heard them say.

"Lewis and I were in on a million-dollar bank robbery," he went on. "And after it was over Lewis took off with all the dough. Thought he could get away with it in that plane of his. I'm the only one in the gang to catch up with him. And now," he finished, "I'm going to do some double-crossing of my own. . . . Eddie, you know what I want you to do?"

Eddie didn't say anything. Through a break in the clouds, the moon now contributed to the weirdness of the scene, painting the four figures with a mysterious, unearthly glow.

"That cave you were whispering about," Voxanne said to Eddie. "Take me to it. Even though you were whispering, I got the drift. You know just where those two round rooms in the cave are. You understand the engravings on the two pennies perfectly. Right?"

Eddie still didn't say anything.

"Answer me," Voxanne ordered, jabbing the gun in Eddie's direction.

"That million dollars," Chip said. "Is that what

Lewis has been looking for all this time?"

Voxanne ignored the question. "Are you going to behave, Eddie?" he asked angrily. "Or am I going to have to get rough?"

Eddie shrugged. "I'll take you to the cave. Why not?"

"No tricks," Voxanne warned. "I wouldn't advise you or your pals to try anything funny. You're three against one," he continued, shifting the gun slightly, "but just remember that I've got this."

Eddie led the way. He moved methodically and silently. Voxanne, walking behind the boys, kept them covered with his gun.

When they passed the crevice where they had seen the bones, Chip was reminded of the paleontologist. He asked, "Is Beestrom a member of the gang, too?"

"How much farther, Eddie?" Voxanne asked, ignoring Chip.

"Not much," Eddie answered.

"We heard Beestrom and Lewis fighting," Chip went on. "And that's why we thought—"

"Well, you thought wrong," Voxanne said irritably. "Lewis hasn't liked the way Beestrom's been poking around for those bones of his. He's told him off more than once. Frankly, I was as worried as Lewis that Beestrom might stumble across that million dollars."

"Is all that money in bills?" Chip asked.

"Let's keep moving along instead of asking so many questions," Voxanne said, nudging Chip with his gun.

They were moving down a fairly wide passage in the cave, Voxanne still behind the three boys.

Eddie stopped abruptly.

"What's the matter?" Voxanne asked, suddenly apprehensive.

"You said you heard all that we were whispering about," Eddie said. "So I suppose you heard me say that tonight I was going to clear up the mystery."

"So?" Voxanne said impatiently.

"If I'm taking you to a million dollars," Eddie told him, "we rate something. The least you could do is answer the questions we have."

"And if I don't?" Voxanne asked menacingly. The words hung heavily in the air for a long moment. Then, surprisingly, Voxanne said, "Okay, okay. Give me your questions, and I'll answer them. What was it that you wanted to know, Chip? Whether the million is in currency? Well, it is."

Jack turned toward Voxanne. "What did Lewis do," he asked, "hide the money in the cave after he crashed?"

"Turn around and keep going," Voxanne said. "We can talk while we walk."

"Okay," Eddie said. "That's okay with me. But before we get going, tell me one thing. Why all of a sudden did you decide you'd answer our questions?"

All three boys were watching Voxanne now, waiting for his answer.

Voxanne smiled. "Why'd I say I'd answer your questions?" he repeated, obviously stalling for time.

"Right," Eddie snapped. "But you don't have to tell me now. I know why."

"Golly!" Chip gasped with sudden realization. "I do, too! What does he care about answering some questions? Soon as we take him to that million dollars, he knows he's going to get rid of us!"

"Now wait a minute!" Voxanne exclaimed. He turned to Jack and Eddie. "You don't believe what he just said, do you?" Before they could possibly answer, he spun back to Chip. "Where'd you ever get an idea like that? From TV? What do you do, spend all your time watching crime shows on TV?"

"Why are you surprised Chip said that?" Jack asked. "Look how you're keeping us covered with that gun."

"Yeah," Eddie chimed in. "That's cornball. It's in all those old movies."

"Fellows, the only reason I've got this gun, believe me, is because I've got to keep you in line." Voxanne

was fairly pleading with them to believe in his inno-
cence. "Would I, *I* ever do what Chip suggested?" He
laughed sarcastically as he answered his own question.
"Of course I wouldn't."

"And what you just did was cornball, too," Eddie
said. "The bad guy trying to scare the good guy and
having a swell time doing it."

"Let's get going," Voxanne said with sudden irrita-
bility.

"No!" Eddie shouted. "Why should we take you to
that million dollars if you're going to do what Chip
said?"

"Eddie," Jack said, "calm down. We don't have any
choice."

"Why don't we?" Eddie demanded. "We don't have
to do what he says. A lot of good it's going to do him
if he shoots us now. He'll never get to the money then."

"I don't want to hurt you boys," Voxanne pleaded.
He gave Eddie a friendly smile as he added, "And I
won't."

"How do we know you won't?" Eddie asked.

"Yeah," Chip said. "What proof have we got?"

To show them that he meant what he said, he began

a detailed recital of all that had happened. That Lewis was ruthless, but that he himself wasn't, was the implication. After Lewis' plane crashed, Lewis had crawled away. From a vertical opening he had glimpsed the underground waterfall. Because of the helicopter that Lewis saw coming to his rescue, he had had to hide the stolen million dollars in a hurry. Keyed up as he was when he concealed the money in the cave, he had vividly remembered what he had seen. During the long, sleepless night he had spent in the hospital, for his ankle was painful, he had engraved the cave's salient features on the two pennies. It not only gave him something to do, but it allayed his worry that when he went for the loot he might not be able to find it.

The boys had been absorbed by Voxanne's account. But now Chip interrupted to ask, "Why did he use two pennies?"

"Why?" Voxanne said. "For the simple reason that it was easier for him to do the engraving on twice the amount of space. Not that Lewis isn't a first-rate engraver. He's done work for a jeweler and for a counterfeit ring. But you have to remember that he didn't have his tools. All he had was a scalpel he'd lifted from the hospital supply room. He did all that line engraving with just that scalpel. I've done some engraving myself, and I've got to admit Lewis is good. You've got to be good to do something like that."

Voxanne went on to explain in detail how Lewis had made the engraving. To hold the pennies immobile while he worked on them, Lewis had fastened them to a night table with a ring of thumbtacks. Though Lewis didn't have a burin—the right engraving tool for the job—he still managed to engrave the lines the same width and depth from beginning to end. He made the O's—of the dumbbell or bone shape—with the scalpel, just as he would have done them with a burin. He made the left-hand curve of the O from the top down and the right curve from the bottom of the O upwards.

"You're probably wondering," Voxanne went on, "how I happened to have one of the pennies. Well, I made Lewis give me one. That way, I'd have half of the directions. That would keep Lewis from double-crossing me again. But I knew my having one of the pennies wouldn't really keep either of us from cheating. He might not need both pennies to locate the place. What I really wanted one of the pennies for was for that trick I pulled on you guys. If we hadn't gone exploring together, I would have found some other way to let you see it."

Having apparently come to the end of his story, Voxanne paused. "Well," he finally said, "haven't I leveled with you? Now, Eddie, don't make it necessary for me to get rough. You can see that Lewis was determined to get that money, and so am I. Now move!"

"As far as I can see," Eddie said, "you just had a good time hearing yourself talk."

Voxanne didn't say anything for a long moment. But then in a surge of anger he ordered Eddie to stand against the wall. "You've been asking for this!" he yelled at him. "Asking for it *all along!*"

Instead of doing what Voxanne ordered, Eddie braced himself. He was determined not to budge.

Infuriated, Voxanne rushed toward Eddie. Jack moved as quickly, yelling to Voxanne to wait.

"Please, please," he begged Voxanne, "let me talk to Eddie! Just for a minute! That's all!"

Voxanne didn't like the idea, but grudgingly he told Jack to go ahead.

The three boys walked out of earshot.

"I don't care what you say," Eddie told Jack, "that guy—"

"I know, I know," Jack interrupted consolingly. "I don't go for him either. But we've got to use our heads. Be quiet now and listen. We can't stand here gabbing forever. He's not going to let us."

"I just wish he didn't have that gun," Eddie said.

"But he *has* got it," Jack snapped. "That's why we've got to play along with him for now—until we get a chance to gang up on him. Now, Chip—"

"Hurry it up!" Voxanne growled.

Jack looked up, nodded briefly, and then went on talking, but more quickly, urgently. "Chip, I don't want you doing anything crazy. You'll just get yourself shot!"

"I know what *I'd* like to do," Eddie said. "Shove him down that big hole under the waterfall. Before long we'll be coming to it."

Voxanne called to them again.

"Remember, Eddie," Jack said hurriedly as they started back, "play it cool! Take it easy, for crying out loud."

Chip halted abruptly. Nervously, he shifted the waterproof bag he was carrying. "Eddie," he whispered breathlessly, "that hole you were talking about shoving him into. Does Voxanne know it's there?"

Eddie shrugged. "How would I know?"

"I bet he does. I bet that's how he's figuring on getting rid of us! It'll be hours before Eddie's father finds that note. By then—"

"Now don't *you* get in an uproar!" Jack told his brother. "You're as bad as Eddie."

"I'm calm," Eddie said. "I'm calm as anything. What we've got to do, Chip, is dump whozit down that hole before he has a chance to dump *us*."

The procession proceeded quietly after that. Not a word was spoken. The silence was broken only by the echoed sounds of their footsteps. The boys led the way, with Voxanne and the gun behind them.

"Are those bats?" Voxanne asked suddenly, breaking the long silence.

They had just passed into a large room. Voxanne was peering toward the ceiling. The boys looked up, searching the domed stone ceiling with the beams of their flashlights.

"There wouldn't be any bats in here now," Eddie said. "They sleep during the day, not at night."

The room expanded in width. The floor up ahead was covered with boulders, the result of an old cave-in that had made the ceiling even higher at that point. Climbing over the boulders was difficult.

"You're sure this is the right way?" Voxanne asked suspiciously. But the next instant his tone of voice changed to awe as he said, "Now, isn't that something?"

Ahead of them was a gigantic stalagmite formation. It rose from the floor of the cave like a shaggy, heavily fluted column and rose and rose until the top of it was lost in the gloom of the ceiling.

"That looks kind of familiar," Chip said.

"To me, too," Jack said. "It's because I've seen pictures of those things in magazines and books."

"Let's go!" Voxanne ordered, hurrying them forward.

"Wasn't there something like that on one of the pennies?" Eddie asked.

Chip shrugged. "Was there?"

"Look!" Jack exclaimed. "Do you see what I see?"

They were passing other stalactites and stalagmites,

arranged in exactly the same pattern as those engraved on the pennies. A constant murmur caused them to pause. They immediately realized the sound was being made by a waterfall. And that meant they were at the end of the trail.

"There she is!" Voxanne said delightedly, as the light from the boys' flashlights spotlighted the water-fall.

So eager was Voxanne to get the money that he passed Jack and Chip and then Eddie. As he rushed forward, he substituted a flashlight for the gun.

"Now's our chance to escape!" Chip gasped. "Come on! Come on!" He turned and started to run. His camera equipment bumped at his side. "Let's go!"

"Have you flipped!" Eddie hissed, afraid Voxanne might hear. "Who wants to escape!"

"The gun's in his pocket!" Jack exclaimed.

"Right!" Eddie snapped back. "So now we can jump him! This is our chance, while he's all excited about getting that money!"

"Then let's go!" shouted Jack.

Overwhelmed by their excitement, Chip ran along with his brother and Eddie.

18 *Lost in the Cave*

The cave's circular room seemed very small after the vastness of the room they had just left. As soon as they entered, they could see the corridor. It led to another circular room, much larger, with a foamy white curtain of water cascading down the far wall and disappearing into a hole.

"Where is he?" Chip asked as soon as they entered the first circular room. They swished the beams of their flashlights around the empty room.

Eddie and Jack didn't have to answer, for the sound of Voxanne's running feet echoed through the corridor. They also saw the bluish light of his carbide lamp as it came bobbing toward them.

"We going to jump him now?" Chip asked excitedly.

"Don't do anything crazy!" Jack warned his brother.

What Eddie had in mind wasn't clear. Saying nothing, he ran forward to meet Voxanne. Jack and Chip followed right behind him.

Voxanne yelled hysterically as he ran. "The money's gone! It's gone!"

However, by the time he reached the boys, he was collected and there was a cold, mean glitter in his eyes. Now the gun was in one hand, his flashlight in the other.

"Lewis beat me to it," he said. "But he's not getting away with the dough this time." He lifted the gun higher, as though in readiness.

"Lewis couldn't have found the money," Jack said.

"Why not?" Voxanne snapped. "It's gone."

"Lewis had supper at the house last night," Jack said. "And he didn't go out. He went to bed. I'm sure of it."

"Yeah," Chip said. "If he'd had the money, he'd have been sure to run off. Wouldn't he?"

Voxanne wasn't completely convinced. He asserted

that they didn't know Lewis the way he knew him. Nevertheless, he began looking around.

He pointed to the spot where the money should have been—according to the engraving on the pennies. "And it's not there, is it?" he asked angrily.

"Here's something I don't understand," Chip said. "In the shape Lewis was in after that plane crash, how could he ever have gotten the money this far?"

"He didn't come the way we came!" Voxanne barked at Chip. "The cloudburst must have closed up the opening he crawled through. That's what's been giving him all the trouble, finding another way to this spot. He told me he hadn't crawled more than a couple of feet."

"Oh," Chip said. "I get it now."

"I'm glad you do." Voxanne was in a foul humor. "Come on, come on, let's get moving. I know my way out of here, so I don't need you. But I want to get to Lewis fast, and I don't want to go making mistakes."

They started to leave the circular room.

Chip turned to Voxanne, who was once again bringing up the rear. "What do you need the gun for?" he asked. "You're not going to meet Lewis down here."

"Just keep going," Voxanne answered cryptically. "I wouldn't try any tricks if I were you. Just keep going—fast."

Every now and then Voxanne snarled at them to hurry.

Not long after they had passed once more through the big room, they entered a dead-end chamber. They had obviously gone the wrong way.

"I hope you're not trying to be funny," Voxanne told Eddie.

"Who's trying to be funny?" Eddie demanded angrily. "We must have missed that narrow passage."

"Yeah. Yeah. I know." Voxanne was suspicious. "But how?"

"I don't know how it happened! I want to get out of here as much as you do!"

In retracing their steps they became more confused. They arrived at a pool of water they had never seen before.

"I don't like this!" Voxanne growled.

"Well, don't shout at me!" Eddie shouted. "So we're lost."

"Are we really?" Chip asked.

"Don't you guys believe me either? It's not a trick or a gag. We're lost, for crying out loud, *plain lost!*"

Eddie's earnestness must have convinced Voxanne. "Okay," he said. "So let's get un-lost in a hurry! I'm not letting Lewis get away with *this* double cross!"

A few minutes later Jack and Eddie found themselves slightly ahead of the others. Eddie whispered, without turning his head, that he had suddenly realized how they had lost their way. At one point there were two elevations. Instead of taking the top one, as they should have, they had taken the lower one.

"What we have to do now," Eddie continued to whisper excitedly, "is not to let on that we know how to get out. You can see this delay's eating at him. He's worried that Lewis is going to beat him out of that money again. A good thing we've got this nylon rope with us. A chance to tie him up is bound to come."

Just as Jack was about to speak, Voxanne shouted. He also waved for them to come to him.

"Let's not do anything wild," Jack whispered as they headed toward Voxanne.

"We'll play it by ear," Eddie answered.

Voxanne had a plan. "We'll never get out of here

at this rate," he said, "so we'll go off in pairs and search for the right exit route. Eddie can be my partner." With a grim smile he added to Jack and Chip, "Keeping Eddie with me will be like insurance. It'll keep you from trying anything reckless. Now, don't go too far off. And, remember, I want you to keep in touch from time to time."

As soon as Jack had a chance, he told Chip that Eddie knew the way out of the cave. He also told him what Eddie was planning to do.

"Hey, that's neat!" Chip exclaimed.

"Shhh! You want Voxanne to come running?"

"What do we do, Jack?"

"We've got to have a good story to tell him. You heard what he said about checking with him. He'll probably want a rundown on where we've been and what we saw."

"Let's see a lot of stuff then," Chip said offhandedly.

"It's a good thing Dad doesn't know about all this. That's all I can say," said Jack. "It's bad enough having to tell him about it afterwards."

They came to a foot-wide diagonal crack that ran from the floor to the ceiling. Chip said jokingly that he would squeeze into it, if it weren't for genuine carbon dioxide fumes—the kind Voxanne had pretended to have met up with.

Jack said, "I doubt if I'd even fit in sideways."

As he spoke, Jack stood up to the crack to compare its width with the width of his body. And that was when he saw the traveling case, half in and half out of the crack.

"Look, Chip!"

Both Jack and Chip directed the beams of their flashlights on the case. It was made of khaki-colored metal with reinforcements at each corner.

"Is it the money?" Chip gasped.

Jack got down on his knees and hurriedly lifted the clasps on each end of the case. The center catch wouldn't move. "It's probably locked," he said.

He tried moving the catch sideways, instead of up and down. Immediately the lid flew open, pushed up by the pressure of the neat bundles of money that tightly packed the case.

"Wow!" Chip exclaimed. "A million dollars!"

Jack whistled, amazed by the sight.

"This would buy just about anything," Chip said,

still staring at the green bundles of money, laid as evenly in the case as bricks in a wall.

Jack suddenly sprang to his feet. "We had better forget we ever found this!" he said excitedly. "That money's poison! We're through—once Voxanne finds us with it! He'll toss us down a hole," Jack said, snapping his fingers, "just like that!"

19 *Fair Exchange*

"Well, we—we can't just leave the money here," Chip stammered. "Can we?"

"Why not hide it?" Jack answered. "Come back for it—you know, whenever we can."

"But this is a million dollars." Chip bent forward to emphasize his statement. *"A million dollars!"*

"Right! And if Voxanne catches us with it, he's not going to mind pitching us in that hole and making off with the money. No! Not one bit!"

Chip went down on his knees and started closing the case hurriedly, resolutely. Forcing the lid down far enough so the clasps would work wasn't easy. Jack knelt beside Chip to help him.

When they almost had it, Chip said, "If we left this here—"

"Wait till—we get this—closed," Jack interrupted. "Push down on it with your knee. We can't let Voxanne find us here like this."

Chip continued to help close the case, but he also went right on talking. "Leaving a million dollars in a cave is too risky. All sorts of things could happen to it. I'm for passing the case off as part of my camera equipment, getting it out of the cave, and turning it over to the police."

With the word "police" he snapped the last clasp in place. They stood up.

"That scheme would never work," Jack said. "Voxanne saw the stuff you had. He's not dumb."

"Well, we can't stand here gabbing either," Chip said. He picked up the case. It was clear he intended to take it out in spite of what Jack had said. "We've got to get back."

"If you do the wrong thing," Jack said, "it isn't just your neck, you know. It's mine—and Eddie's, too."

There was a rattling sound as of someone coming.

"Voxanne!" Jack exclaimed. "I expected him to be coming after us. We've been gabbing away—"

"Shove it out of sight!" Chip ordered, pointing out the case with the beam of his flashlight. "I'll go take a look!"

Chip started out fast. But when his imagination peopled the dark ahead with who-knew-what waiting to spring on him, he walked more slowly and cautiously. Another rattling sound made him move even more slowly. Then, just ahead, he saw a rubble heap. It must have been freshly formed, for dust rose in the beam of Chip's flashlight and an occasional stone still moved erratically down the crest of the heap. Other stones rumbling down could have made the rattling sounds.

"It was a rockslide we heard," Chip said when he returned to Jack. "And nobody was around to set it off. That's just one example of what I was talking about. If we left that million, it could be buried in a rockslide. It'd be good-bye forever then to that dough."

They recovered the case from the crack in the wall where Jack had temporarily hidden it.

Jack said, "You still think that Voxanne isn't going

to notice you didn't have that case before?"

"Jack, he's concentrating on one thing—that million. I'm telling you, you could walk around on your hands and he wouldn't know the difference."

Nevertheless, Chip emptied the waterproof bag in which he carried his films, stuffing the films into his overall pocket. He removed the shoulder strap from the bag and snapped it onto the case that held the money.

"I'll leave the bag here," Chip said. "Maybe Voxanne did notice the strap. So when he sees it, everything will look just like it was before. Okay?"

"Okay," Jack said. "Let's go."

"I'm surprised you're not raising a row," Chip remarked as they started off.

"If you run into a stone wall," Jack answered, "you don't keep on doing it, do you? Not if you've got any sense."

"I'm not stubborn," Chip said. "I'm smart."

They were surprised to find Voxanne and Eddie practically in the same spot where they had left them.

"We just went down that damp, back-breaking tunnel and came back," Voxanne explained. Then he asked, "Did you have any luck?"

Jack stood in front of his brother to keep Voxanne from seeing the case. "I didn't see anything familiar," Jack said. "Not a thing that we'd passed coming in."

Chip made a point of stepping in front of Jack. He didn't want Voxanne to think he was trying to hide something. "Jack's right," he told Voxanne. "We drew a goose egg."

"Tough," Voxanne exclaimed disappointedly. "You were taking so long, I figured you—"

"There was a rockslide while we were looking," Chip said. It was a detail to make their search appear genuine.

"That held you up?" Voxanne asked.

"You have to remember," Jack said, "that we covered a lot of territory."

"And you can't go rushing around in a cave," Eddie offered in defense of the boys. "You do, and you might find yourself going down in space."

"We'll stick together from here on," Voxanne said. "Before we start, I want to say I'm sorry about a lot of things I said. I am. I mean it."

This sudden change in Voxanne's attitude rendered

the three boys absolutely speechless.

"How about letting me give you a hand with your load?" Voxanne said to Chip. Voxanne reached out with both hands and grabbed the money case. "I want to prove to you I meant what I said."

The strap kept Voxanne from getting possession of the case. It also gave Chip the chance to clutch the case with both hands.

A tug of war began.

"Let me have it," Voxanne begged Chip in a surprisingly friendly way. "Come on. I mean it. Really!"

"Aw, no!" Chip objected, desperate to keep Voxanne from getting the case. "It's my camera stuff. I need it."

"That's what held you up so long," Voxanne argued. "Lugging that thing."

Chip shook his head. "It's not heavy."

"Let Chip carry it," Eddie told Voxanne. "He needs the exercise."

"He won't even let me touch his junk," Jack added, worried that Voxanne might become suspicious over Chip's insistence on keeping the case. "Just because it's his junk. That's the only reason."

"Well, the reason I'm set on helping Chip," Voxanne

said, "is to prove to you guys that I'm sorry about the things I said. And I want to do it in some concrete way." He smiled. "I'll tell you what. How about a compromise? Open up that thing, and we'll divide all the stuff in it. That way none of us will have a lot to carry. I know you say it's not heavy, Chip. But it's still a load. And I think we ought to all pitch in and—"

Voxanne stopped because Chip was hastily removing the strap from his shoulder. Obviously Chip preferred to have Voxanne carry the case rather than let him get a look at its contents.

"What a production," Eddie grumbled. "And just over who's going to carry what."

"Well, it's settled," Voxanne said. "Go on. You, too, Jack and Chip. Lead the way. How about taking that tunnel? We haven't been down it."

Chip strode ahead of all of them. Jack kept close to Eddie. He wanted to tell him that the money was in the case Voxanne was carrying and that he should stop pretending he didn't know the way out of the cave and get them out. But Voxanne kept so close to them that Jack didn't have a chance to speak to Eddie.

Finally Jack became desperate. As they were passing

through an immense room, dripping with stalactites, he stopped. "I thought of something," he said.

They all waited for him to explain.

"You know where those two levels are, Eddie?" Jack went on. "Maybe that's where we made our mistake. We took one when we should have taken the other."

Eddie stared intently at Jack, his brow furrowed. It was obvious he couldn't understand why Jack would be revealing the way to get out of the cave.

"What do you think?" Jack asked Eddie.

Before Eddie had a chance to answer, Voxanne started to laugh. He laughed hard, hugging the case with the million dollars in it.

"What's so funny?" Eddie asked.

Voxanne had difficulty talking, he was laughing so hard. "What a time you had, Jack," he managed to say at last, "trying to talk to Eddie." He laughed again. "And you couldn't because I kept right on your heels. You'd found the money. What you wanted to do then was tell Eddie it was time you stopped fooling around and got out of the cave. And you couldn't, could you?"

"What do you mean, we found the money?" Chip protested.

"And what a time *you* had," Voxanne said to Chip with a fresh burst of laughter. "You didn't want to give up this case. Oh, I'll say you didn't. And I let you go on thinking I didn't know what was in it."

"You know?" Chip gasped.

"Of course. I knew all along. And it's all mine. A beautiful million dollars!"

20 *Underground Encounter*

"How'd you ever know?" Chip asked, puzzled.

"You can't figure it out, huh?" Voxanne said, still in wonderful spirits because he had the money, and now he was sure they were not really lost. "How about you, Jack? Eddie?"

Jack shook his head—not in answer to Voxanne's question, but in disgust. "I told you he'd recognize that case," he said to Chip.

"You didn't say that," Chip objected. "You were just afraid he'd notice I hadn't had it before."

"That case belonged to me," Voxanne said. "Not only did Lewis hijack the million bucks, but he swiped that case of mine. And I'm telling you, searching around the way I was doing, the picture of that case was right there in my thoughts like on a TV screen. So as soon as I saw this"—he slapped the case suspended from the shoulder strap—"I knew you'd found it."

"We should have hidden it," Jack muttered.

"All right," Chip admitted. "I was wrong. Golly, everybody's got a few mistakes coming to him."

"What was that about two levels?" Voxanne inquired.

"What do you mean?" Eddie asked.

"You know what I mean. Jack as good as admitted that you know how to get out of here."

"Oh, that," Eddie said disparagingly. "I don't know anything about two levels. The guy's dreaming."

Voxanne turned to Jack, his high spirits gone. "Well?" he demanded. "What've you got to say?"

Jack shrugged. "It was just an idea," he said weakly.

"You three work like a team, don't you?" Voxanne said angrily. "Now you want to keep me down here because I found this." He slapped the case again. "That's not smart."

The boys fidgeted uncomfortably, saying nothing. After a long pause, Voxanne smiled. It was plain he was going to try another approach. "Listen, fellows," he said, and the hand that had slapped the case before now rubbed it soothingly. "You know what's in here. One million smackeroos. A million! *One million!* So you get me out of here on that upper or lower level or whatever it is, and I'll treat you right. You'll get some of this good green money—green as the fields in spring." He laughed at what he had said. The laugh was plainly meant to convince them that he was a friendly, generous person. "How about it?" he asked after a moment.

"But that's stolen money," Chip said with emphasis. "You said so yourself."

"I'd get you out of here," Eddie told Voxanne. "And I wouldn't want anything for doing it. But—but—"

"You don't know the way. That's what you're trying to say." Voxanne broke in on him, angry again. "You think I'm fool enough to swallow that lie?"

Sudden sounds caused them all to tense. Someone was approaching. Then they saw two bobbing carbide lights off in the darkness.

"That might be Pop!" Eddie gasped.

"And if it is," Voxanne snapped nervously, "that's Lewis with him."

The bobbing lights were rapidly drawing closer and closer.

"Just remember," Voxanne warned them. "I've got the gun in my pocket. You're covered, all right. So no funny stuff. There are enough bullets to take care of all of you, Lewis included."

As the others waited silently, their eyes on the approaching lights, Voxanne said, "I'm not dumb, you know. I knew all along why you didn't want to take me out of the cave.

"You were right, too," he added. "You think I'd let you get away from here alive, so you could squeal on me?"

"Boy," Chip said, expressing extreme disgust. "And when you offered us that stolen money, you weren't going to—"

A skirmish in the darkness interrupted Chip. It took him a moment to realize what had happened. Eddie had yelled, "Pop!" and it was clear he was trying to warn his father of danger. Before Eddie could yell anything else, Voxanne had rushed up to him and jabbed the gun into his side.

Eddie's warning shout had been mistaken for a

greeting. There were return shouts of "Hello, there!"

"That doesn't sound like Pop!" Eddie exclaimed immediately.

"Beestrom?" Chip's voice rose questioningly. "Could it be him?"

They all kept the beams of their flashlights directed straight ahead. Finally the light reached the approaching figures.

"You're right, Chip," Jack said.

"Yeah!" Chip exclaimed happily. "It *is* Beestrom!"

"Man, what a relief!" Eddie sighed. "I was sure it was Pop, walking straight into this mess!"

"This doesn't change things," Voxanne reminded them. "The gun's in my pocket, but remember, I've got it on you all the time."

In the cave, Beestrom looked even more like a Frankenstein monster. The light from the lamps highlighted the bones of his face, making his cheeks seem all the more sunken. The young fellow with Beestrom was so much shorter that the effect was almost comical.

"We're lost," Voxanne told Beestrom. "Can you tell us how to get out?"

"I don't think I could possibly tell you," Beestrom

said in his cultured tone. "But that's hardly necessary. To make sure *I* could depart, I marked all the turns and forks. You'll see the marks. I used removable markers."

"Wonderful!" Voxanne was delighted.

"Just continue in the direction from which I came," Beestrom said. "You'll see the first mark. It will be a—yes, yes, a right turn."

Voxanne herded the boys in front of him and prepared to start off.

"If you should have any trouble," Beestrom said as he was about to move on with his companion, "Lewis might help you."

The mention of Lewis brought Voxanne to an abrupt halt. "Lewis?" he said in a sharp voice.

"He's up ahead." Beestrom stood still, half turned in their direction as he spoke. "I ran into him. He's still annoyed with me for intruding. I don't know what he's looking for, but I'm certain my work is as significant as his."

"We found some bones!" Chip blurted out. "Eddie says they're Indian, because there's a green color on top of the skull. They're probably a very important scientific discovery."

Beestrom moved back to them. "Indeed," he said, intensely interested.

"Yeah," said Chip. "Do you want us to take you to the bones?"

Before Beestrom could answer, Voxanne sternly reminded the boys that they were going with him. Then he added, for Beestrom's benefit, that he needed them.

As Beestrom walked off, he said, "Perhaps you can take me to those bones another time. Incidentally, I had no luck whatsoever with that clue on your penny. I was just at the place. I happened across it by accident. At least, I think it's the place. You'll be coming to it."

No sooner did he begin to move away from Beestrom, than Voxanne turned back toward the scientist. The boys stopped, also.

"You know another way out?" Voxanne asked Beestrom. Frantic as he was to get out of the cave with the money, he didn't want to risk running into Lewis.

Beestrom shook his head. "Remember, I had to use markers. Otherwise I wouldn't be able to find my way to the outside world."

After leaving Beestrom, Voxanne became increasingly jumpy. Once, when a stone was dislodged, he accused the boys of trying to tip Lewis off that they were coming.

He demanded that they walk faster. He also insisted that they shouldn't make a sound.

When they came to the first of Beestrom's marks, Voxanne rubbed the mark out. It infuriated him that Eddie and the boys objected.

"I don't *want* Beestrom getting out of the cave!" he yelled at them. "He'd be a witness against me, wouldn't he?"

"That's terrible," Chip said, aghast that Voxanne would do such a thing.

"It's the lowest," Jack said.

"Watch what you're saying," Voxanne warned them. "Just move along. And be quiet about it."

"Let's not go," Chip said.

"He's not going to shoot us." Jack planted his legs far apart, as Eddie had done when he had refused to budge. "If he does, Lewis'll hear the shots and come running. And he's scared of Lewis!"

"Move!" Voxanne shouted.

"No!" Chip shouted back. "Go ahead and shoot if you want to!"

"Fellows, cut it out," Eddie said.

"You'd better!" Voxanne warned them.

"Push him too far," Eddie went on, "and we'll all end up getting shot."

"Come on, move!" Voxanne ordered.

Both Jack and Chip grumbled. However, Eddie had convinced them to cooperate with Voxanne. But each time they came to one of Beestrom's marks along the route and Voxanne erased it, the boys became angry all over again.

"Go ahead and shoot!" Jack yelled at Voxanne, just before they reached the circular room again. "He's not going to, Eddie. He's too scared of Lewis. Shooting us would let Lewis know where he is. And he's scared—"

"I'm not scared of that double-crosser!" Voxanne shouted hysterically. "Why do you keep saying I am?"

"Because you are!" Chip yelled back.

"Lewis would take that million from you!" Jack shouted. "That's why you're scared!"

"He's got you all jittery," Eddie joined in, realizing that the boys' plan was to unnerve Voxanne completely.

"I'm not afraid of him!" Voxanne shrieked. *Him—him—him* echoed tauntingly from the rock walls.

Voxanne had his gun out now, swiveling it from side to side. He was ready for Lewis no matter from what part of the darkness he might spring. Somewhere ahead of them, settling earth caused a few stones to make a rustling sound.

"Lewis!" Voxanne exclaimed, and shot at the sound.

"He's shooting back!" he cried wildly as the echo of his own shot resounded from the distance.

Voxanne ran forward into the circular room. In the corridor ahead, he saw the light of a carbide lamp. At the same moment, a beam of light from the corridor stabbed through the darkness and illuminated Voxanne and the money case in his hand.

"Stop right there!" Lewis' voice lashed out at them.

A gunfight between the two criminals started then. Their carbide lights, in the darkness, pointed each of them out as targets.

On impulse, Chip took out his camera and began recording the scene. He kept the camera shutter open in the virtually complete darkness. The film was exposed only by the gun flashes, together with what little light there was from the carbide lamps and flashlights.

Immediately after one of the shots, Lewis let out a howl of pain. Jack turned the beam of his flashlight on him. Lewis was standing completely exposed to view. He held one hand with the other, twisting about in pain.

As soon as Voxanne realized he had shot the gun from Lewis' hand, he started to lift his own gun slowly and carefully for the final shot.

"Drop your gun!" a voice behind Voxanne ordered. "I've got you covered!"

Voxanne whirled about, shooting. But he was shooting at emptiness! There was no one behind him.

Before Voxanne could turn around, Lewis sprang

forward and clamped a bear hug on him. They wrestled wildly, frantically. Lewis tried desperately to keep his hold, so that Voxanne wouldn't have a chance to shoot.

They careened into the corridor, bouncing from one wall to the other. They progressed in this way to the second circular room.

Eddie and the Power boys followed, keeping their flashlights turned on the struggling pair. Chip continued to take pictures. He was using his electronic flash now.

Suddenly something streaked by them so fast that they didn't know what it was. Then they saw that it was Blaze! He was leaping up again and again at Voxanne and Lewis!

"Blaze!" Jack and Chip shouted. "Come back!"

Blaze ignored their shouts. Jack ran forward to get him, but he was stopped by the horror of what he saw.

In their frantic struggle over possession of the gun, both men had stumbled into the hole beneath the waterfall. And the money case went down with them!

Jack, Chip, and Eddie raced to the waterfall. Ignoring the spray from the falls, they sent the beams of their flashlights down into the bottomless hole.

"There they are!" Chip cried out.

"I see them!" Eddie exclaimed. "On that ledge!"

"Talk about luck," Jack said. Without turning around, he ordered Blaze, who was nuzzling him from behind, to go away. "Lewis! Voxanne!" Jack yelled down to the men.

There was no answer.

"You think they're all right?" Chip asked.

"Maybe they weren't so lucky after all," Jack said. "In a fall like that, you can break your neck. We've got to—"

"The money!" Chip suddenly moved the beam of his flashlight about frantically. "It went down with them. But it's not on the ledge. Do you see it?"

"Take it easy," Jack said.

"But we'll never be able to get it out of there if it went all the way down!"

"No," Jack said. "Not out of there."

"You act as if it's nothing!" Chip exclaimed. "That was a million dollars, man! I ought to kick myself. If I'd only listened to you and hidden that money—"

"I told you to take it easy," Jack said, grinning. "I did hide it."

"You what?"

"You know where we found the case," Jack explained. "That's where I hid it. And I put some rocks and stuff in the case, about the weight of the money. Remember when you went off? You went to see what that noise was all about. That's when I had my chance."

"Wow! Did you really? . . . I believe you, but—"

Beestrom and his companion came rushing into the circular room. They said they had heard the explosions and had followed the sounds to find out what was happening.

"What's going on?" he asked. "What happened?"

Jack explained that what Beestrom had heard were gunshots. Then, briefly, he told him what had occurred.

"I'll venture to say," Beestrom said, "that Lewis used ventriloquism to trick Voxanne into turning around. How else can that voice behind Voxanne be explained? And no one being behind Voxanne when he turned?"

"But is Lewis a ventriloquist?" Chip asked.

"He told me he was," Beestrom answered. "That I'm a paleontologist seemed to disturb him. To show me— for the sake of his ego, I guess—that he, too, had a profession, he spoke of his ventriloquism. He said that he once was a ventriloquist in a carnival."

"Hey," Jack exclaimed, "that's the answer!"

"What're you talking about?" Chip asked.

"Lewis didn't have to use electronics to get all those spooky effects. And when that so-called spirit said, 'Don't shoot!' it was Lewis. That wasn't much different from what happened just now when Lewis threw his voice and told Voxanne to drop his gun."

"What we've got to think about," Chip said somberly, "is how to get Lewis and Voxanne up out of that hole."

Jack nodded. "Hmmm. And about lugging them out of the cave."

Suddenly there was the sound of a hurried approach beyond the corridor.

"Sounds like a lot of people," Jack said, puzzled.

"And how!" Chip exclaimed.

They all stood facing the corridor, waiting to see who was coming. Blaze began to bark excitedly, the sound magnified by the confined space.

"Quiet, boy!" Chip said, as he grabbed for the dog's collar.

But Blaze broke free of Chip's grasp. He shot forward into the darkness toward those who were approaching.

22 *A Lucky Penny*

Chip and Jack ran after Blaze.

They were halfway down the corridor when they saw men entering it from the other end. All of the various lights confined within the limited space made the corridor quite bright.

Two policemen were in the lead—with their guns drawn. Mr. Rowans came next. Blaze passed them both and jumped and barked at a man bringing up the rear. At first the boys didn't recognize him.

When they saw that he was their father, they ran up to him almost as fast as Blaze had done. They had to push the dog away in order to greet their father. Blaze continued to jump and bark.

"When did you get back, Dad?" Chip asked.

"Are you all right?" Mr. Power looked at Chip and then at Jack. "Those shots—"

"What's going on here?" one of the policemen asked.

Jack and Chip began to tell the policemen about the gunfight over money that had been stolen. Eddie had come down the corridor and was talking to his father.

"I arrived none too soon," Mr. Power said. "I see that."

"Didn't you get the note we left for you, Pop?" Eddie asked his father.

Mr. Rowans shook his head. "I was worried. That's why I called—" He indicated the policemen with a movement of his head.

"Well, I wrote a note," Eddie said defensively. "And I left it on the kitchen table."

Chip had started to tell his father about the pictures he had just taken, when one of the policemen exclaimed, "What was that?"

They all stood motionless, listening. At first, the only sound was the steady whispering of the waterfall. Then a shout suddenly broke through. It was gone so quickly, it seemed unreal. If there were echoes, they blended into the sound of the falls.

"Come on!" Chip exclaimed and started running toward the waterfall. "That must've been Lewis or Voxanne!"

Mr. Rowans had brought a rope ladder with him, thinking he might need it to rescue his son and Jack and Chip. The ladder was lowered into the hole. Lewis came up first, with a safety rope around him, secured by a bowline. A few minutes later Voxanne appeared at the top of the ladder.

Aside from Lewis' hand, and his ankle, which had been injured again, both men appeared to be all right. They were, of course, drenched by the spray from the waterfall. They said they had been so stunned by the fall that for a time they couldn't speak.

Lewis hobbled about and winced occasionally. Still he managed a grin, meant to be friendly.

"You're surely going to recover that money," he said to the policemen, who still had their guns drawn.

Chip was about to say the money wasn't down in the hole. However, a long habit of speaking too soon caused him to glance at his brother, as though for a go-ahead.

At that precise moment Jack volunteered to go down the ladder for the money.

"For the money?" Chip exclaimed in spite of himself.

"Sure!" Jack answered with emphasis. "What else would I be going down for?" And as he moved to look down into the hole, he added, "I'm just wondering about the ladder. I mean, how close to the bottom it goes."

"Forget about the ladder," Mr. Power told Jack. "I'm not letting you go down there. It's certainly a good thing I arrived when I did."

"There's no need for him to go," Lewis said. "But there is a million dollars involved here—you know that."

Jack and Chip asked Lewis questions—and so did the police. Lewis answered all of them in a most cooperative and friendly way. Voxanne remained silent. It seemed as if Voxanne and Lewis must have agreed, while they were down in the hole, that when they were rescued Lewis would do all the talking.

Lewis revealed that after he had left the hospital he hadn't been able to find the specific cave entrance into which he had gone after crawling away from the burning plane.

"Maybe it was covered by a rockslide," Eddie conjectured. "That cloudburst caused some slides. Right, Pop?"

Mr. Rowans nodded.

Lewis then explained that he hired Rowans as a guide, describing to him the circular room to which he wanted to be taken. But Rowans didn't know where this room was. The cave was so big, Rowans explained, that there were many parts he had never had a chance to explore.

This was when Lewis had gotten the penny from Eddie. He hoped it would provide a clue which might have slipped his memory and also provide him with the luck he needed. He always carried the two rare pennies with him—as good luck pieces—because they had once served as models for counterfeit "rare" coins from which he had made a great deal of money. When he had only one of the pennies, the other—figuratively speaking—was worth a million. It might literally have been that valuable to him, he said, if it had supplied the information he needed to find the million dollars.

In addition to luck, Lewis admitted in the course of questioning, he needed time. He didn't want an invasion of tourists into the cave, for one of the tourists might have stumbled across the money. That was why, to delay the opening of Rowans' cave, he had made spectral sounds, hoping they would be interpreted as a ghostly reenactment of a murder that had once been committed in the cave.

That the pennies were lucky was again proven by the service they performed when Voxanne showed up and demanded his share of the loot. Lewis had explained to Voxanne what had happened, but Voxanne wouldn't believe him. It wasn't until he produced the pennies that he was able to convince Voxanne that his story was on the level.

"And I guess if it weren't for those lucky pennies," Lewis concluded, "you boys wouldn't have gotten involved. And you wouldn't have written the note I picked up off the table this morning. It told me exactly where the place in the cave was I'd been trying to go to all along."

"You see," Eddie said to his father. "I told you I wrote a note."

"We shouldn't have left it on the table," Chip said. "That's where we goofed."

"Man, we sure did goof," Jack agreed. "How'd we ever do it? I mean, being suspicious of everybody the way we were."

"But I figured Pop would be down in the kitchen first," Eddie said defensively. "He's always down before it's even light outside."

Lewis had his wallet out. "How about making a deal? You see, I still believe, in spite of all that's happened, that those pennies are lucky and that they're—"

"Are you trying to bribe me?" one of the policemen demanded, grabbing Lewis' arm.

"Of course not," Lewis said. "I'm not talking about a penny-ante bribe. I'm talking about a million-dollar *deal*. What I've got in my hand here is just a down payment. I've been cooperative with you in answering all your questions. Now if we all work together and get that money up out of there, even splitting it up ten ways there'll be plenty for all of us."

"The money's not down there," Jack said flatly, pointing at the hole.

Chip grinned. "It sure isn't."

Lewis and Voxanne looked completely bewildered.

"You played tricks," Jack said, justifying what he had done. "Both of you. All that ventriloquism." Jack turned to Voxanne. "And the way you pretended that time that you'd passed out, just to hear what we'd say. So to keep you talking," Jack continued, looking directly at Lewis now, "and answering questions, I let you think the money was down there in the hole."

"But it did go down," Lewis said, still bewildered. "I know it did. I was holding it."

"Yeah," Jack agreed. "Yeah. You were holding the *case*."

"And that's *all* you were holding," Chip chimed in delightedly.

"I'd taken the money out," Jack explained, "and put it in a good, safe place. That cloudburst had washed the case right to a good hiding place. And that's where the money is—right now."

Mr. Power came hurrying down from the attic in Mr. Rowans' farmhouse. He had used the attic as a darkroom for developing the pictures Chip had taken.

As he put the prints, one by one, on the round kitchen

table, he exclaimed proudly, "Take a look at these, would you!"

Beestrom, Eddie, Mr. Rowans, and Jack and Chip crowded around the table.

"Hey, Chip," Jack said, "they're neat."

"I've got to agree with you." Chip laughed. "They came out pretty good."

Beestrom nodded solemnly and said, "Very artistic."

"That's it exactly," Mr. Power said excitedly. "But they're more than arti—"

"They're real cool," Eddie said.

"Yes, yes," Mr. Power agreed with Eddie. "And they're also dramatic! Just look at this." He pointed at the eerie shots that Chip had taken of the gunfight. Streaks of light emerged from shadowy figures and crisscrossed blackness. "This will make a terrific picture story. I've been traveling all over for just this kind of a story."

"And when this story breaks, Eddie," Jack said, "your—"

"Of course!" Eddie exclaimed, overjoyed. "Pop's cave is going to get terrific national publicity."

In the midst of all their excitement, the phone rang.

Chief of Police Kerner in Pine Springs was calling to congratulate Jack, Chip, and Eddie and to thank them for helping with the recovery of the stolen money. He also wanted to tell them that they would undoubtedly have a sizable reward coming to them.

Eddie immediately said he was going to use his reward to make additions to his coin collection.

"And I'm going to start a coin collection," Chip said.

All the happy excitement finally got to Blaze. He started to bark, looking from one smiling face to another.

"He's not afraid of caves anymore," Jack said. "That's what he's trying to tell us."

"Could be," Chip agreed. "Then again, he might be thinking of starting a lucky coin collection, too."

THE POWER BOYS

The Mystery of
THE HAUNTED SKYSCRAPER

The Mystery of
THE FLYING SKELETON

The Mystery of
THE BURNING OCEAN

The Mystery of
THE MILLION-DOLLAR PENNY